HER FAVORITE REBOUND

CIDER BAR SISTERS, BOOK 4

JACKIE LAU

First edition: March 2022
ISBN: 978-1-989610-26-8

Editor: Latoya C. Smith, LCS Literary Services

Cover Design: Flirtation Designs

Cover photograph: Adobe Stock

$$[\ 1\ ]$$

Sierra Wu was a mess.

This wasn't new, however, since she could never seem to do things quite right. The disapproving looks of her mother and grandmother were a testament to this fact.

She checked her jacket to see if a pigeon had pooped on it—like that infamous day three years ago—but there was no bird poop. Nor was there any lipstick on her cheek like last time, when she'd shown up late thanks to the TTC.

Today, she'd allotted herself tons of time for transit issues, so of course there hadn't been any, and she'd arrived early for dim sum. Yet her family was still unhappy with her.

Story of her life.

Po Po, the matriarch of the family, radiated more disapproval than usual—an impressive feat. Ninety-two years old and several inches shorter than Sierra's five foot two inches, she could strike fear into the heart of anyone.

Sierra couldn't help envying her friend Nicole, whose po po made TikTok videos and teased her in a loving way and didn't think she was a complete failure. Sierra's grandmother was nothing like that. She probably had the same complaints as usual:

Sierra was divorced and childless, and she didn't have a proper career.

Sierra had tried. Oh, she'd tried so hard to be an engineer like her brother. But she'd been very bad at it, and it had made her miserable. She now had a cute little greeting card store in Baldwin Village, which suited her much better.

Auntie Marlene and Cousin Rachel, her family in tow, arrived as Sierra took a seat beside her grandfather.

"Hi, Gung Gung," she said. "How are you feeling today?"

"Sierra." He smiled at her, but that was all.

She tried to remain upbeat. "Do you like my scarf, Gung Gung?" She held it up. "Red. Very lucky, right?"

His hand shook as he reached out to touch it. "It's pretty."

She didn't ask about his week. He'd get confused, unfortunately. And while some elderly people might enjoy talking about their past, her grandparents never had. They were one of those immigrant families that kept the past a secret.

Instead, she took out her phone and showed her grandfather something she'd drawn recently. Gung Gung had always been supportive of her artistic interests. Sure, he'd wanted her to do well in school, but he'd also bought her paints and pastels—good ones—and praised her artwork.

"Aiyah, what are you doing?" Ma asked.

Sierra couldn't help feeling defensive, as she often did around her mother. "He likes when I show him my work."

Indeed, Gung Gung swiped his finger across the screen of her phone and looked momentarily confused when a new picture showed up. It was an illustration she'd done of Toronto in the wintertime, a red streetcar in the forefront.

"It's nice," he said.

An ear-piercing scream rang through the noisy restaurant. Sierra's brother Lincoln and his family must have arrived. His baby girl had a huge set of lungs, and his sons, who were four and six, were just as loud.

Once everyone was seated, sort of—Lincoln's kids were struggling with the concept, whereas Rachel's sat like obedient angels —and Po Po placed the order, Auntie Marlene started bragging about Rachel, and Ma started bragging about Lincoln, and Sierra finally noticed that her father wasn't here today.

Good for him for getting out of this, she supposed.

Sierra would never be allowed to do a thing like that, even though she had a job that actually required her to work on the weekends. But she'd hired someone who worked Sundays and occasional Saturdays—like today—so she could trek out to Scarborough to see her family.

It was dim sum. She ought to look forward to it, except...

"He did such a good job!" Ma said. "My light works perfectly now!"

Lincoln grinned as if Ma were talking about him doing something impressive, rather than changing a lightbulb.

Not surprisingly, Auntie Marlene called Ma out. "You're bragging about him changing a lightbulb?"

"He left work early to do it."

"Well," Auntie Marlene said, "Rachel is *too important* to leave work early."

Whereas Lincoln enjoyed praise, no matter what it was for, Rachel always looked vaguely uncomfortable with it. She and Sierra had never been close, but Sierra didn't mind her cousin, even if she made Sierra look bad in comparison. Rachel was a doctor, married to a doctor, and they had three kids.

"What happened to your hand?" Auntie Marlene asked Sierra.

She looked down at her left hand. "I, um, got a bad papercut at work yesterday."

"You're still working at that card store?"

"Yes. I *own* it."

Auntie Marlene looked at Ma and raised her nose in the air. Sierra clearly wasn't as good of a daughter as Rachel, and Ma glared at Sierra for making her look bad.

As usual.

"You got a really bad *papercut?*" Ma asked, as though only Sierra could do something so foolish.

But if it had happened to Lincoln, Ma would have said, *You poor baby.* Then she would have hunted down the offending piece of paper and ripped it to shreds.

And if Sierra had changed Ma's lightbulb, Ma would have told her that she did it wrong or complained that Sierra was too short and needed to go on a higher rung of the stepladder than Lincoln. There was no way to win.

Sierra couldn't wait until tonight, when she'd be free of all this judgment.

The har gow arrived, and she placed two on her grandfather's plate—shrimp dumplings were his favorite—before helping herself.

Sierra's mom turned to her, about to offer a criticism no doubt, but Sierra was saved by one of Lincoln's boys throwing a dumpling across the table and hitting Po Po in the shoulder. Sierra's eyes widened in shock, and Po Po glared at her great-grandchild, who immediately burst into tears.

"Rachel," Auntie Marlene hissed. "You're the doctor. Make sure she's okay."

Po Po, who presumably didn't want to be fussed over, sent Auntie Marlene a stern look.

"Ma. Please let her check."

However, Auntie Marlene backed down as Po Po's look grew even sterner.

The water chestnut cake and turnip cake came next, and Sierra busied herself with serving her grandfather.

He thanked her and said, "Where is your husband today?"

Her heart sank. He'd apparently forgotten that she hadn't had a husband in years. Seeing him suffer from dementia was tough. Should she make excuses for her ex not being here, or mention her divorce?

"He's working," she murmured.

They'd been speaking quietly, but Ma still heard.

"You need to find a husband soon," she said, clucking her tongue. "You're getting wrinkles around your eyes. Looking old."

Yet some people still thought Sierra looked very, very young. So young that she got carded at the liquor store, even though she was thirty-four and the drinking age was nineteen.

"You should ask Rachel about her skincare routine," Auntie Marlene said. "She has perfect skin, doesn't she? And she's five years older than you."

"Wah, Rachel's skin isn't perfect." Ma did occasionally leap to Sierra's defense when Auntie Marlene sang Rachel's praises, though in private, Ma would compare Sierra unfavorably to her older cousin.

Yeah, Sierra couldn't wait until her date tonight. A quiet dinner at a French bistro, a movie…and they'd have the theater all to themselves because her rich boyfriend could afford shit like that.

Her family didn't know about her boyfriend, even though she'd been dating Colton for over a year. It was a pain to tell her family stuff like that, but she'd tell them eventually. When she really, really needed to improve their opinion of her.

"If only your ex-husband didn't turn out to be gay." Auntie Marlene reached across the table to pat Sierra's hand.

"At least he had a good reason to divorce her," Ma shot back. "Sierra didn't do anything wrong, but *you* are different. Your ex-husband—"

"Justin isn't gay," Sierra said. "He's bisexual." No matter how many times she explained it, it never seemed to make it through their heads. "I knew that when we started dating. Sometimes things don't work out, that's all."

"But he has a husband now," Ma protested.

"He's *bi*, like I said, and his husband had nothing to do with our separation—they didn't meet until later."

Her mother couldn't stand the fact that she was divorced, but Sierra would much rather be divorced than married to someone like Rachel's husband, for example. The man might be a doctor, but from what Sierra could tell, he was a lousy father and husband.

Instead, she had a nice ex-husband. They were better off as friends, and she hadn't been heartbroken when her marriage had ended. Disappointed, yes, but relieved at the same time.

"Are you still hung up on him?" Auntie Marlene asked with fake kindness.

"No." Sierra managed to restrain herself from stabbing her har gow with her chopstick.

"But still no boyfriend?"

"I know what you need, Sierra," Ma said. "A makeover."

"Ah, you're right, that's exactly what she needs!" Auntie Marlene said.

Rachel shot Sierra a sympathetic look.

Sierra was more than a little alarmed at this makeover plan. First of all, her mother and aunt were agreeing, which was nearly unprecedented. Would Auntie Marlene make Sierra look hideous so Rachel would continue to be the superior daughter?

Sierra wouldn't put sabotage past Auntie Marlene, though it did seem somewhat unlikely. No, her aunt and mom might genuinely try to help—which was also scary. Their sense of fashion was, well, the opposite of Sierra's.

Po Po nodded. "She could use a makeover."

Oh no. Her *grandmother* thought she needed a makeover? Po Po's approval of this plan meant it would almost certainly happen.

"There's nothing wrong with Sierra's appearance," Rachel said.

Auntie Marlene seemed horrified that her daughter was disagreeing with her elders.

This was why it was impossible to hate Rachel. She took

breaks from being perfect to stick up for Sierra, which made her even more perfect.

Ma ignored Rachel. "I will get you an appointment with my hair stylist next Saturday," she said to Sierra.

"Ma, I have to work."

"You're trying to get out of this, but I won't let you. Your auntie and I will come down to your *store*"—she said this with disdain—"and drag you out."

Lincoln was laughing. Bastard.

Sierra's brain suddenly conjured up an image of her dressed like her aunt, with a weird perm and fake brand-name clothes and...

Yep, Sierra needed to bring out the big guns. It was time.

"I don't need a makeover to find a man," she said. "I already have a boyfriend."

Ma seemed hopeful; Auntie Marlene looked skeptical.

Po Po continued looking stern.

Sierra was actually excited to see the look on her family's faces, particularly her mother's. "I'm dating Colton Sanders."

"*The* Colton Sanders?" Ma asked, much like how Sierra's friends had reacted.

"Yep. I assume you've heard of him?" Sierra smiled as her mom's mouth dropped open.

"Isn't he a billionaire?"

"That's right. I'm dating a billionaire."

"Wah, Sierra," Auntie Marlene said. "I thought you were better than this. Making up outrageous lies?"

Sierra pulled out her phone and passed around a photo of her and Colton together.

"Did you Photoshop this?" Auntie Marlene asked. "It doesn't look like your body."

"Yes, it does," Ma said.

"Her boobs look too big."

"Flip to the next photo," Sierra said, ignoring the conversation about her boob size. "Do you really think I Photoshopped multiple photos of me and Colton Sanders? I can call him right now, if you like."

She hoped her auntie wouldn't take her up on that. Colton was likely busy and didn't want to be disturbed.

"Is it true he owns a private jet? An island in the Caribbean?" Ma asked excitedly. "It's been such a long winter. I could really use a holiday."

See, this was why Sierra had waited to tell her family about Colton. She'd even asked him to ensure no pictures of them together ended up in the press. He'd said he'd take care of it—and he had.

"Calm down, Ma." Lincoln was sulking.

Well, he got praise for changing a lightbulb, and if Sierra had a kid who'd thrown a dumpling at her grandmother, she would have been in deep shit, which Lincoln had been spared even though he put zero effort into parenting. He left it all to his wife, who currently had her hands full with a fussy baby.

"Yes, Colton does own an island," Sierra said. "I haven't been there. Yet."

"I still don't understand how you're dating a billionaire," Auntie Marlene said. "You have wrinkles around your eyes, as your mother said. Surely a man like Colton Sanders could get anyone he wanted."

Trust family to make her feel bad.

But Sierra expected her mother would stick up for her now, and she wasn't disappointed.

"Wah, I was exaggerating," Ma said. "I told Sierra she would have wrinkles around her eyes *if* she wasn't careful, but she looks good now, and I'm sure Colton Sanders can afford all the nice facial masks for her."

Ma looked at Sierra with pride...because she happened to be dating a rich white guy.

Once again, Sierra turned her thoughts to her upcoming date.

For dinner, at her request, they weren't going to have a private room. Colton had a tendency to rent out the entire restaurant, but that wasn't something she needed regularly, as she'd told him, slightly embarrassed by the frivolousness of it all. But when he'd suggested renting out the small VIP theater, she hadn't protested. Getting him to change his mind on the restaurant was enough.

Besides, the movie was a special occasion.

It was *her* movie.

Well, she had the same name as the main character. That was all.

Unfortunately, since the book series had begun several years ago, it had become a big hit, and people were always making comments about it to her. As she'd told her friend Amy, it was like being named Bridget Jones or Alice in Wonderland.

The first time she'd heard of the urban fantasy series, it had been a funny coincidence, but by the time the second book hit number one on the New York Times bestseller list, she was sick of it. In the past couple of years, she'd tried to embrace it and laugh about it because what else could she do?

The fictional Sierra Wu wasn't a mess. She wasn't divorced, nor did she own a greeting card shop, nor did she ever get pigeon poop on her jacket or lipstick on her cheek. Blood, perhaps, from the demons she slayed, but never lipstick or pigeon poop. She kicked ass and had saved the world on more than one occasion.

Sierra Wu, the real person, sure hoped the fate of the world never rested on her shoulders.

She was certain she'd fail.

Though right now—for once—nobody was calling her a failure. But Sierra couldn't fully enjoy it. First of all, because the questions from her family would never stop, and second of all, because it wasn't really about *her*.

"Of course it is," Ma said.

Oh, shit.

Sierra realized in horror that she'd spoken out loud.

"It is about you," Ma said. "To catch a man like him, you must be very beautiful and talented, which you are."

Yep, now Ma was calling her beautiful and talented when she would have laughed at those words being applied to her daughter not ten minutes ago.

Sierra tried not to roll her eyes and busied herself with pouring more tea for her grandfather. When she gestured to the steamer with the har gow, he nodded, and she placed one on his plate.

"Aiyah!" Auntie Marlene said. "He shouldn't have so much salt."

Dim sum was a terrible choice for someone watching their salt intake, but also...

Gung Gung could eat whatever the hell he wanted. If Sierra made it to ninety-four, she wouldn't hold herself back from an extra dumpling.

Nor would she now, for that matter. She picked one up with her chopsticks and stuck it straight in her mouth.

Gung Gung nodded at her approvingly. She wasn't sure he'd caught the whole Sierra-is-dating-a-billionaire part of the conversation, but that was fine. Unlike certain members of her family, he'd never been chronically disappointed in her, even if he might be a bit hazy on the details of her life now.

So when one of Lincoln's demon children launched some siu mai across the table, toward Gung Gung, Sierra's reflexes sprang into action. She not only managed to prevent the siu mai from hitting her grandfather—no, she caught it in her hand.

Unfortunately, because she was still a bit of a mess, she also managed to dip her sleeve in the dish of chili sauce and mustard. No way would this have happened to Rachel.

Yeah, sometimes life wasn't fair, but at least Sierra was looking forward to this evening.

~

"How was dim sum?" Colton asked.

Sierra looked up from her menu. "I told my family about you."

She surreptitiously adjusted her navy dress, regretting her uncomfortable outfit choice even though she looked pretty hot. She'd allowed her boyfriend to cover the cost of a personal shopper and several new outfits that were fancy enough for their dates.

"Yeah?" he said. "How'd that go?"

He didn't look nervous about her family's opinion of him. When you were a man like Colton, the world bowed down to you. He came from a wealthy family—the one percent of the one percent.

Sierra's family was upper middle class. Her parents had paid her university tuition, and she'd grown up with advantages.

But not ones like Colton had.

He graced her with the cocky smile of a man who moved smoothly through life, and she returned his smile.

Colton Sanders was six feet tall. (He claimed he was six-two but had once confessed to her that was a lie.) He had perfectly tousled brown hair that looked good even when he'd just rolled out of bed. (Totally unfair.) His eyes were almost shocking in their blueness, and his abs were rock hard (How? She had no idea. But they were perfect, though she'd once drunkenly admitted to Nicole that it made him less comfortable to cuddle.)

Yep, Colton was a rich, good-looking, man, and he'd picked *her*. He was the first boyfriend who'd truly made her feel special. Something her parents never did, that was for sure.

She leaned forward, but before she touched his hand, his phone buzzed.

"Shit," he muttered. "I have to take this." He stood up and walked toward the washrooms.

This was one of the downsides of dating Colton Sanders. Sure, he had lots of people to do things for him, but there were many things he liked to oversee himself.

Sierra read over the menu and tried to figure out what to get. She was still training herself not to care about price when Colton was paying—he was a billionaire, so she shouldn't feel guilty for a forty-dollar main course—but old habits died hard. After all, Sierra didn't make a lot of money herself, and she did have to worry about cost in the rest of her life. Colton would have been happy to help her out more, but she refused, and he found this... admirable and quirky. Or something like that.

Yes, she didn't come from his world, and occasionally, she was confused as to why he was with her, but he was always quick with his reassurances.

By the time she decided on the pan-seared scallops with warm lentil salad, Colton still hadn't returned. That was okay, though. She could handle being left alone at a restaurant table for fifteen minutes because her boyfriend was on the phone.

She gazed out the window and sipped her wine as she tried to push aside the odd discontent in her heart.

$$[\ 2\ ]$$

Jake Tong didn't believe in love at first sight, not until it happened to him.

It was a cold February evening when he arrived at the restaurant in downtown Toronto. He was treating Lewis, who'd recently gotten his dream job, to dinner.

Jake didn't pretend to understand why working for this particular company was Lewis's dream job as an environmental engineer. But he was trying with his brother these days, he really was, so when Mom had mentioned Lewis's career success—of course, Jake hadn't heard it from his brother directly—he'd texted Lewis, suggesting they do something to celebrate.

To his surprise, Lewis had agreed.

Jake knew he appeared calm as he was shown to his table, but inside, he was a teeny-tiny bit nervous.

Lewis and Victoria hadn't arrived yet. Although Jake used to practically live in suits, he wasn't accustomed to wearing them now. He wiggled his shoulders, trying to get comfortable, then decided to drape his jacket over the back of his chair. He also rolled up his sleeves before picking up the menu. If he remembered correctly, the lamb was quite good here and—

Oh.

Oh.

Out of the corner of his eye, he noticed an East Asian woman sitting alone at a table, resting her chin on her hand. And then he had a ludicrous thought.

That's the woman I'm going to marry.

He shook his head. Why was he thinking such a thing? He didn't even know her.

Yet the thought persisted.

It wasn't merely lust. Lust at first sight was something with which he was intimately familiar. He'd been attracted to many, many women over the years. Slept with a good number, too, back in the days when—

Well. He tried not to think about that part of his life.

This woman was beautiful, definitely. He could only see her side profile, but she had a hint of a smile on her face as her gaze dropped to the menu, and that slight smile was nearly enough to take his breath away. Long black hair, elegantly pulled back. When she ran her thumb up the stem of her wineglass, he was already imagining her touching his skin instead. He figured she was about his age, maybe a few years younger.

He couldn't explain it, but there was just something about her, and he *knew*. His heart pounded as he looked at her, yearned from afar.

It was her. It had always been her.

He swallowed some water and prepared to go over. If you were in love with a woman, it was only sensible to actually talk to her, even if nothing else about this was sensible. But somehow, this feeling seemed to transcend time and space and knowing the other person's name and occupation.

Just as he was about to stand, a white man approached her table and kissed her cheek before taking the seat across from her.

A chill passed through Jake's body.

This woman appeared to be on a date. That was bad enough. But the man she was with?

Colton Sanders, Jake's arch enemy.

It was doubtful the feeling was mutual. Colton probably didn't think about Jake enough these days to consider him an enemy. Probably didn't give him much thought at all.

There was, however, a silver lining: this would make it easy for Jake to get an introduction.

He stood up and walked to the table where Colton and his date were seated.

"Hello, Colton," Jake said, pleased with himself for not adding, *You absolute fucking bastard.* "It's been a while."

Colton got to his feet. Standing, he was four inches taller than Jake.

"Hey." Colton gave him a slap on the back, as though they were old friends.

Which…they were.

"How have you been?" Colton asked, putting on a bit of a show, as he always did.

It took Jake a moment to answer because he was looking at Colton's date, now that he was only a few feet away. She had big dark eyes, and she wore a sparkling navy dress that showed off her shoulders.

"Uh," Jake said. "I've been fine." He'd spent much of the past two years alone in his house near the Danforth, unsure what to do with his life, but he was fine. "Aren't you going to introduce me to your lovely date?"

"Of course." Colton smiled. "This is Sierra Wu, my girlfriend."

Jake almost sputtered. Colton had an actual girlfriend? Rather than banging everything that caught his fancy?

Well, he was probably still doing that, too.

Colton seemed to enjoy Jake's shock. Jake glanced down and ran her name over and over in his mind. *Sierra, Sierra, Sierra.* It was pretty, and her last name—oh, she had the same name as the character in that new movie. He didn't comment on it, since she was probably sick of hearing about it.

"A pleasure to meet you, Sierra," he said.

He almost let out an unhinged laugh, feeling like someone was playing a trick on him. The one time he'd fallen in love instantly, and she was already in a relationship…with his enemy.

Jake knew he had to warn Sierra away from Colton. There was no way Colton could be a good boyfriend, and given Colton's past behavior, the fact that she was Asian made Jake even more uncomfortable. Her name…

Was that why Colton was dating her? For the novelty of that?

Jake returned to his table and didn't even bother trying to read the menu. It was taking all his effort not to stare at Sierra and Colton.

When she went to the washroom a few minutes later, he got up again. He might seem like a creep waiting for her in the hallway, but she needed to hear what he had to say.

After she exited the single-stall washroom, she took a few steps before he said, "Sierra."

She paused, looking at him with suspicion. Her dress hugged her body, and it took him a moment to find his voice again.

"Don't date Colton," he said. "He's a terrible guy."

"What do you know about him?" she asked, one hand on her hip.

"I used to work for him. I was one of his lawyers." Shame coursed through Jake, but he wouldn't dwell on it now. "I did some of his dirty work—not all of it, of course, because he needs a whole team of people for that. He calls you his girlfriend, but don't believe him. I've never known him to have a girlfriend before, and I can't imagine him actually committing to anyone."

Something flashed across Sierra's face, and when she spoke again, her words were angry. "We've been together for over a year. Why do you look so shocked? You think I'm not good enough for him?"

Jake's head was spinning. "Quite the opposite. I just warned you off dating him, didn't I? You're too good for him."

She let out a peal of laughter as though he'd told a very funny joke, and that laughter set him on edge. She shouldn't find this hilarious.

"I mean it," he said. "You are."

Sierra felt like Jake was in her personal space, even if he wasn't all that close to her. Maybe it was because of the intensity in his eyes.

He was spouting nonsense, though. Sierra Wu wasn't too good for Colton Sanders. Nobody would think that.

Except Jake's words seemed genuine, and she had the strange sense that he saw her differently than anyone else ever had.

When her cheeks heated, his lips twitched.

How infuriating.

Infuriating that he'd noticed her blushing.

Infuriating that he was so damn handsome.

He had light brown skin, a touch darker than hers, and cropped black hair, and his eyes…oh, his eyes.

No, she would not drown in them.

His eyes were thin and dark, and his jawline was magnificent, if it was possible for something like a jawline to be *magnificent*.

Yes, fine, she found him attractive. Sue her. It wasn't a crime to find someone attractive just because she had a boyfriend—she certainly wasn't going to act on it, and besides, she still thought Colton was the better-looking guy.

But she flushed even more as Jake leaned forward slightly—and that felt wrong.

She swallowed and backed up against the wall. "I'm not too good for Colton."

"Sierra," Jake said, and she mentally kicked herself for enjoying the way he spoke her name. "He's a piece of shit."

"Are you envious of his success?"

"No. He's succeeded because he's privileged and has no morals. I've seen how he treats women, and it's not good."

"He treats me just fine," she said, lifting her chin. "Perhaps he's changed."

"I used to be a bit like him."

"Have you changed?"

"Yes, but—"

"You see?" she said. "There's no reason he can't do the same."

"He has a disturbing fetish for Asian women."

"I've seen no signs of that. Just because he's dating me doesn't mean—"

"I know him well. He's carefully crafted the image he's shown you."

"And you think you're so perfect?" she shot back. "Here you are, chasing after another man's girlfriend."

"I'm not chasing after you." He leaned against the wall opposite her in the hallway, putting a little more physical distance between them, but the way he was looking at her…it was enough to make her pulse kick up.

"Your eyes tell me otherwise," she said without thinking.

"Do they?" He spoke softly, and it felt like his breath was caressing her skin, which was a ridiculous notion, especially since he wasn't all that close. Then he sighed. "I just want you to be careful, okay? Colton is powerful and has no scruples. I can't say, of course, that he's cheating on you, but it wouldn't surprise me."

"He's taking me to a movie tonight. We'll have the theater all to ourselves."

"It's easy for him to throw his money around."

"I—"

"Just be careful," Jake repeated. He gave her one final look before returning to his table, and it practically seared Sierra's skin.

She slumped against the wall, needing a moment to recover.

What the hell was that? Why had Jake's presence affected her so much?

After composing herself, she returned to her table. Colton was checking something on his phone, but he set it down a moment later and turned his smile to her. Unlike Jake, whose lips barely twitched, Colton had a winning smile.

She didn't tell him that she'd spoken to Jake privately. What would be the point? Sure, Colton had his faults, but he was good to her, and it wasn't like she was going to act on anything Jake had said.

Nope, she'd put that encounter out of her mind and have a fun night.

[3]

SIERRA HAD BEEN RIGHT: Jake had been chasing after another man's girlfriend. Yes, he'd wanted to warn her, but he also wanted her for himself.

He sighed. Was he still an asshole, no better than Colton?

Yet he continued to have the feeling that she was the person he was meant to marry, though maybe he'd wake up tomorrow and wonder what the hell was wrong with him. Love at first sight? Really?

When he returned to his table, Lewis and Victoria were just sitting down.

Dammit. He hadn't been able to greet them properly.

"Who were you talking to?" Lewis asked.

"Just an acquaintance," Jake replied, trying to play it cool and hoping Lewis didn't notice that Colton fucking Sanders was in the restaurant.

Lewis wouldn't be impressed by the coincidence. He'd hated Colton for much longer than Jake had, for all the environmental damage his properties had caused. For his treatment of First Nations. For…

The list went on and on.

Lewis was the oldest child. The good kid, who'd always gotten top marks in math and science. He'd won a province-wide science fair in high school, and their mother still kept the trophy in a position of pride. He'd also never been swayed by money and power, which was why he and Jake had frequently butted heads as adults.

Jake wanted to get back to the way they'd been as teens. They might not have been best friends, but they'd gotten along and had each other's backs.

Victoria had been Lewis's university girlfriend, and though they'd been together for fifteen years, they still seemed very much in love. Not in a showy way, but even Jake, who was far from an expert on such things, could tell.

"Thank you so much for inviting us out," Victoria said to Jake.

He smiled at his sister-in-law. "You're welcome." Then he turned to his brother, who was sitting across from him. "You deserve it after all your hard work."

When Lewis didn't immediately reply, Jake stiffened. Perhaps this dinner had been too ambitious. Perhaps they wouldn't be able to spend an evening together without someone leaving in a huff.

But then Lewis managed a quick, "Thank you," and Jake thought they might be able to get through tonight.

As long as Lewis didn't notice Colton.

So even though Jake was tempted by Sierra, he did his best to focus on Lewis and Victoria and steer the conversation away from any topics that might prove to be landmines. But he couldn't completely stop himself from looking her way.

A good man like Lewis wouldn't yearn for a woman who was in a relationship.

An hour and a half later, they finished dinner. It ended up going not too badly, though it was still awkward with Lewis. And when Jake asked for the bill, the waiter smoothly informed them that it had already been paid.

Some power move of Colton's, Jake guessed.

"Uh, yes," he stammered. "I paid earlier when I went to the washroom. You know, in case my brother tried to fight me over the bill at a dinner in his honor. But it's just habit to ask for the bill after the meal."

Jake was usually better at lying, but he supposed he was out of practice.

Luckily, Lewis didn't question it.

When Jake got home, it was ten o'clock, and he cracked open a beer—he hadn't ordered a bottle of wine at dinner, as Lewis didn't drink—and sat on his couch. He tried not to torture himself with thoughts of Colton and Sierra in an empty theater together. Would they actually pay attention to the movie? Would Colton slide his hand up her thigh, under that dress…

Jake had become a master at torturing himself in the past two years. Maybe he deserved it for all the shady shit he'd done.

Sighing, he pulled up Google on his phone. It took a few searches to find something that wasn't about the Sierra Wu urban fantasy series, but eventually, he found a reference to her in the "about" section of a store called Moonbeam Messages. There was also a photo, so he was positive he had the right Sierra.

How on earth had she and Colton met? She didn't seem like the sort of person who ran in Colton's set. No, she owned a greeting card store that also sold washi tape, mugs, and other things. Some of the cards were her own designs, and they were rather whimsical and made Jake smile. He found himself staring at a sloth card for five minutes straight, which was something he'd certainly never done before.

He couldn't help wanting to know more. Had she drawn this on a tablet? Had she done a rough sketch on paper first, her tongue peeking out from between her lips and her brow furrowed in concentration? Had inspiration struck her while she was out for a walk…or taking a shower?

That brought to mind all sorts of delightful images that he had no right to think about.

He was pleased she was a small business owner—like him, sort of—rather than a high-powered lawyer with questionable ethics, or similar.

Like he used to be.

He took a long pull on his beer.

She was just a woman he'd met at a restaurant. A woman he'd talked to for all of five minutes. Five minutes in which he'd been desperately, desperately fighting the urge to whisper in her ear and ask if he could kiss her. Five minutes in which he hadn't failed to notice the goose bumps that appeared on her arms when he got even a little close to her. He suspected they were due to desire, not fear.

Unless, of course, she was afraid of her desire, which wouldn't be unreasonable.

He blew out a breath and chugged the rest of his beer.

Sierra Wu, Master Demon Slayer, hurried through the streets of San Francisco's Chinatown, her white tank top ripped to show even more skin, blood artfully dripping off her face. She appeared to be wearing a push-up bra and was clearly meant to appeal to the straight male gaze.

Aside from the outfit of the heroine, however, Sierra Wu—the small business owner—was enjoying the movie.

She'd read the first book, but that was quite a while ago now, and she couldn't say how closely the movie followed it. She was sure Amy would update her at some point. Amy had seen the movie yesterday—opening day.

The cinematography and special effects were mind-blowing. The storyline was compelling. The love interest, Rebel, was hot.

And Sierra was in an empty theater with a big bag of popcorn, a small cup of Coke, and her very thoughtful boyfriend.

She put down her popcorn, snuggled up against him…and found herself thinking that Rebel looked a bit like Jake, if Jake were slightly beefier and had lots of tattoos.

Actually, Jake could have lots of tattoos that had been hidden by this white shirt. He didn't have any on his forearms, though—the sleeves of his shirt had been rolled up and she hadn't seen any tattoos there.

Why was she thinking about Jake?

Well, she supposed it wasn't every day that someone warned you off dating your boyfriend, but she'd try not to focus on it.

Though when she and Colton were in the car later, his driver taking them back to his large house worth a shocking number of millions, she found herself wondering about the fact that Colton had taken two phone calls during dinner.

She didn't know much about his business; she'd never bothered asking. She just knew he was a real estate mogul—it was impossible not to know that—and he had other things going on, too. But she'd seen how hard he worked, and now she couldn't help wondering…

He pulled her close and started kissing her neck as his hand drifted beneath her dress.

"One sec," she said, pulling back. "I have a question."

"About the movie? I enjoyed it." He returned to kissing her neck.

She laughed. "I'm serious, Colton."

"Okay, okay." He held up his hands. "What's your question?"

"When is it…enough?" That was too vague. She tried again. "Like, you could maintain your lifestyle if you never worked again. What keeps you going?"

He tilted his head to the side. "What brought this on?"

"I was just wondering. I don't know."

"Stagnation is bad. The enemy of advancement. My goals are constantly evolving."

"But why do the goals always involve more money?"

"It's not all about the money," he said.

"I know, but—"

"I like building things. Having a vision and seeing it through."

She didn't know how to articulate her feelings. It was just... something was niggling at her. She wouldn't ask him to be who he wasn't, but it *would* be nice if he worked a little less and her time with him wasn't squeezed in between business trips and meetings.

Then again, aside from the twenty minutes for those two calls, he'd been hers all evening. It seemed like a small sacrifice. Besides, he liked the fact that she wasn't needy.

Now that she thought about it, it did seem weird that her boyfriend was a successful businessman and she knew almost nothing about what he did.

Maybe you're afraid of what you'll find.

No, that wasn't true.

Was it?

But perhaps it was time to do a little research, then ask him more questions. Push aside the voice at the back of her head that sounded suspiciously like Jake.

Yes, even though she'd only met him tonight, for some reason, she could remember exactly how he sounded, exactly how it felt to have his gaze boring into hers.

"You know," Colton said, as he pulled Sierra against him, "I think you should wear the same outfit that Sierra Wu did in the movie."

"Which outfit?" she asked. "The tank top soaked in demon's blood?"

"I was thinking a little earlier, before it was completely soaked."

When she chuckled, he smiled at her in the dim light of the car.

"You look beautiful tonight," he murmured.

She studied his face. His perfect, clean-shaven features. She was a lucky, lucky woman who was living a fairy tale: her boyfriend was filthy rich, and he had a mansion in Toronto and multiple vacation properties, including his own island. He'd arranged for her to get a new wardrobe.

And her family was actually impressed with her for once.

She melted against him and reminded herself that she had nothing, absolutely nothing, to complain about here, yet she couldn't completely silence that niggling voice.

Dammit, Jake!

She hoped she'd forget about him soon.

$$[\ 4 \ ]$$

Sierra sighed in relief as she entered Ossington Cider Bar behind Rose Pang. It was nice to be out of the chilly March air.

Amy Sharpe, Nicole Louie-Edwards, and Charlotte Tam already had a table at the back. Sierra took a seat in between Nicole and Amy.

"Hey!" Amy gave her a hug. "Did you like the movie last weekend? I thought it was good but not as good as the books."

On Tuesday, Amy had sent her a text asking what she'd thought of the movie, and Sierra had been at work at the time… and then she'd forgotten to answer.

"Yeah," Sierra said, "it was enjoyable."

"Or did you not pay attention because you were too distracted by the man beside you?" Amy waggled her eyebrows. "I can't believe you had the movie theater all to yourselves."

"I watched the movie." Sierra paused. "Most of the time."

This was met by chuckles.

"Speaking of Colton," Nicole said, "I thought he was joining us tonight?"

Sierra shook her head. "He had a last-minute trip to New York."

"Right." There was a note of suspicion in Nicole's voice.

"Do you have something against Colton?"

Nicole hesitated. "I don't know him well enough to have anything against him."

Sierra told herself to relax. It was true; her friends had spent very little time with Colton in the past year, which was something she hoped to change soon.

But she was still on edge after last weekend.

Why couldn't she get Jake out of her mind? She shouldn't waste any brainpower on that man, and she certainly wasn't going to tell her friends about him.

Their server came around, and Sierra ordered a cider aged in whiskey barrels, which she'd had before and quite liked—they didn't have it on tap often. She also ordered the Brussels sprouts. They were smothered in cheese and bacon, and they were absolutely delicious.

And healthy.

Ha. Healthy would be a stretch, but there must be some nutritional value in the sprouts.

Her friends didn't understand why Sierra ordered this every time when she could eat cheese and bacon without Brussels sprouts—there was a bacon cheeseburger on the menu, for example. But she really did like the Brussels sprouts themselves. They were cut in half and nicely browned on the bottom… Mmm. She was already salivating.

"How's apartment hunting?" she asked Charlotte. Charlotte and her boyfriend were planning to move in together, and they were looking for a place bigger than where either of them currently lived.

"Ugh." Charlotte shook her head. "Not well. Rent is so damn expensive in Toronto, and the last place we looked at had thin walls."

Nicole choked on her cider.

"I could hear the kids running and screaming next door,"

Charlotte said. "One of them was in the middle of potty training —the mom was yelling about that. And since I work from home…no way. I want walls that don't make me feel like I'm in the middle of someone else's living room." She took a long swallow of her cider. "I'm also cranky—"

"You, cranky?" Nicole said. "Whatever are you talking about?"

Charlotte shot her a glare. "Because I've had to cut back on coffee."

"Who would have guessed that you were drinking too much coffee?"

"Cut it with the sarcasm. I can't handle it today. Apparently, drinking eight cups a day can interfere with your sleep, and I wasn't sleeping the greatest. Getting old sucks."

"I have a bad knee now," Rose said. "Are you supposed to have a bad knee in your thirties? It's only triggered in very particular circumstances, usually involving lots of stairs, but still. I also feel too old for camping. I used to enjoy it every summer, but now I'm like…nah, too much work."

Sierra's cider arrived, followed a few minutes later by her Brussels sprouts.

"Anyone want one?" she asked, not expecting her friends to take her up on the offer.

"I do," Nicole said.

"You? Eat a Brussels sprout?"

"I haven't tried one in, like, three years."

Sierra pushed her plate in Nicole's direction, and Nicole speared a piece of Brussels sprout with her fork. She stuck it in her mouth…then covered her mouth with her hand and lurched forward.

"That was *vile*," Nicole said, still making a face.

"I can't believe I wasted one of my Brussels sprouts on you," Sierra said. "You didn't deserve one."

"You're right. I didn't deserve that." Nicole guzzled some of her cider and laughed. "I'm gonna wait at least five years until I try one of those again. I'll stick with eating, well, pretty much anything else."

Sierra relaxed as her friends discussed nothing in particular, and by the time they decided to head out, she was feeling better than she had in a few weeks. Of course, part of that was due to the alcohol, but mostly it was from hanging out with old friends.

As she took the streetcar back to the Annex with Rose and Amy, Sierra leaned against the window and wondered what would ruin her contentment tomorrow.

Because there would almost certainly be something.

"Sierra!" Ma yelled over the phone.

"Ma, please," Sierra said. "It's nine in the morning on a Sunday."

Sierra had been pouring herself some coffee in the kitchen. She took her mug to the living room and plopped down on the couch.

"I told Cece that you're dating Colton Sanders," Ma said.

"Of course you did," Sierra muttered.

"Ah, why are you being smart with me? I gave birth to you!"

"I know. Twenty-two hours in labor." Sierra sighed. "Second labors are supposed to be faster, but I took longer than Lincoln."

Her mother liked bringing this up, as if it was Sierra's fault for being slow to come out of the womb.

"And you were two weeks late," Ma said. "Nine pounds. So big!"

Yeah, despite being just a little over a hundred pounds now, Sierra had been a big baby, and that was her fault, too.

Another thing she'd heard many times before.

"I went to see Grace's baby yesterday," Ma said. "You should get pregnant. You're thirty-four now, and thirty-five is, how do you say, geriatric pregnancy? Grace is smart. Three kids by thirty-five."

Sierra shut her eyes and tried to ignore the temptation to be snarky.

She and Grace Chau, Auntie Cece's daughter, were only two months apart, and they'd been compared their entire lives. When Sierra wasn't being compared to her brother, she was being compared to Grace Chau. And when she wasn't being compared to Grace Chau, she was being compared to Rachel.

But although Sierra didn't mind Rachel, Grace was a different matter: one of those people who bragged about her perfect life all the time on social media.

And, okay, maybe Sierra also had a hard time forgiving Grace for taking her first steps at eleven months. Before Sierra started walking, even though Sierra was older. Not that Sierra remembered any of this—no, her first memory was of Grace stealing her teddy bear—but Ma liked to bring it up.

"I've told you before," Sierra said, trying her utmost to be patient, "I don't want kids."

"But you haven't given me a reason!"

"I simply don't want children. Isn't that reason enough? Why would you pressure someone who doesn't want kids to have them? Besides, you already have three grandkids."

"When you hold the baby in your hands," Ma said, "you will feel differently. You will love them forever."

"And forever complain about how long I was in labor."

"What did you say?"

"Nothing, nothing." Sierra sipped her coffee.

"Before, I thought you just had to meet the right man, but now, you have him."

"How do you know Colton is the right man? You've never seen the two of us together."

Ma clucked her tongue. "I just have a feeling. I'm your mother, after all. It will be good for you to have a baby with him, even if you split up. Big child support payments."

Sierra couldn't believe what she was hearing.

Well, no. She could.

See, there were reasons she hadn't told her family about her billionaire boyfriend for a year, even though she knew they'd be impressed.

"If you meet him," Sierra said, "and that's a very big *if*, don't you dare make such comments to his face."

Unfortunately, she could easily imagine her mother doing it, despite the warning.

Sierra would have to move to Antarctica afterward. That would be the only option.

"Don't worry," Ma said. "I'll be good."

Sierra snorted. Hopefully Ma couldn't hear that over the phone.

Of course, she wasn't that lucky.

"Sierra!" Ma shouted. "I'm very happy for you, you know. I get to brag. Cece was impressed, but I think she was a little doubtful that it was true. Can you send me a picture?"

"No. I don't want it to be all over the internet within an hour."

Ma actually laughed. "Yes, that's exactly what Cece would do, I understand."

Wow. Ma was being reasonable.

"That's why you must come to Scarborough next Saturday," Ma said. "You can show pictures to Cece in person."

So much for thinking her mother was reasonable. "Ma, I can't take every Saturday away from the store. I told you."

"Why do you need that silly store now? You're dating a billionaire."

Sierra gripped the arm of the couch.

Yes, the store didn't make a lot of money, but it still made enough for her to live on.

And it was her dream.

She'd defended herself a million times before. There was no point saying anything now; Ma just didn't want to understand.

Sierra sighed. "I need to go. I have lots of things to do. Laundry, grocery shopping—"

"You should get Colton to hire a maid for you."

"I'm hanging up now."

Sierra was massaging her temples when Rose walked downstairs. They lived together in an old Victorian house, which Amy had inherited from her great aunt. Sierra had met Amy when she'd responded to Amy's ad for a roommate. She'd been desperate for a place to stay because the apartment she was supposed to move into had burned down—not her fault, but just part of being Sierra Wu, Certified Mess. (The fact that it wasn't her fault hadn't stopped her mother from blaming her for it, of course.)

Amy had since moved in with Victor, her husband, who owned the house next door. Rose had decided she didn't want to live alone anymore, so she'd become Sierra's housemate.

Although this whole living arrangement had started with a fire, it had turned out not too badly for Sierra.

"Something wrong?" Rose asked as she stopped by the couch.

"Just a phone call with my mother." Sierra didn't provide details. "I'm going to the grocery store and probably the liquor store. You need anything?"

"No, I'm good," Rose said.

Sierra got ready to brave the unpredictable March weather with her uncool cart, the kind used by grandmas in Chinatown. She didn't go to Chinatown for groceries today, though. She went to the nearest chain supermarket before making a quick stop at the liquor store to stock up on wine and soju.

"Can I see some ID, please?" asked the clerk.

Even though this happened nearly every time, Sierra still groaned inwardly. She reached for her wallet and pulled out her driver's license.

Yes, she knew they were supposed to ID anyone who looked under twenty-five, but she'd hoped to be done with this hassle by the time she was thirty-four, even if some women would take it as a compliment to be carded all the time.

Sierra didn't like it, though. First of all, because it felt like nobody saw her as a proper adult, and second of all...

"Your name is Sierra Wu?" the clerk asked.

That.

She was tired of it.

"It is." She didn't know why he needed clarification. It was right there on her damn driver's license.

"I saw the movie on Friday," he said. "It was *so* good."

He was a white guy of maybe twenty. For some reason, she had a feeling he was the sort who'd mainly been impressed by the breasts and skimpy blood-covered clothes of Sierra Wu, Demon Slayer.

"I can't believe you're more than a decade older than me," he went on.

She was so not in the mood for this today.

At least he hadn't questioned whether her ID was real and gotten his manager involved. That had happened to Sierra once at a super sketchy bar.

"Why do Asian girls age so well?" he asked.

"Uh, could you ring up my wine, please?"

He did as requested, though he shot her a *why-are-you-being-so-rude-I-thought-Asian-girls-were-meek* sort of look. How annoying.

"Thank you," she said crisply after he placed her purchases in a paper bag. She walked out into the cold March weather, determined not to slip on some black ice and break all her bottles, like she'd done earlier this winter.

When she arrived home safely, she found her roommate in the kitchen. Rose was positioning her stuffed alpaca, Fred, so it looked like he was drinking from a mug.

Sierra sold a small number of stuffed animals at Moonbeam Messages, including this particular model of alpaca, which Rose had recently purchased. She'd tied a pink ribbon around his neck; Sierra wasn't sure whether this was a permanent addition, or whether it was just for the photo shoot.

"I made an Instagram account for Fred's adventures," Rose explained.

"He's starting the day off right with a cup of coffee. What's he going to do next?"

"I won't post another picture for a couple of days, so I have time to figure it out."

Sierra held up the bottle of peach soju that she'd bought. "He could drink this?"

"What if he gets a wicked hangover?"

"True. I hear alpaca hangovers are particularly brutal."

Sierra put her food and booze away. She was in the middle of preparing an early lunch when her phone buzzed.

Hey, babe, Colton said. *Sorry about last night. Have a good time with your friends?*

Yes, but we missed you, Sierra replied. *Still in NYC?*

Returning today. Want to come over for dinner? I'll send a car around to pick you up at six thirty, how's that? Just tell me what you want to eat.

After responding, she sent him a few kisses and set down her phone with a smile.

And then, for some reason, she found herself mentally composing a retort to Jake. *You see? Colton treats me well.*

Ugh, why was he popping into her head? Why?

Being an adult was certainly different than Sierra had imagined as a kid. First of all, the world had changed quite a bit in the last twenty-five years. She'd thought they might travel in flying cars; she wouldn't have predicted they'd possess phones that were amazing cameras.

Second of all, she hadn't expected Ma to keep bugging her and judging her quite so much—though really, she should have known better.

She'd also never imagined she'd be divorced and have a roommate at this age. She'd thought she'd own a house. Ha! Real estate was completely unaffordable in Toronto now.

And when she'd been a kid herself, it had been hard to imagine not becoming a mom one day, but she'd figured it out by the time she was twenty.

She never could have predicted she'd have the same name as a character in a movie. Though it wasn't really the same surname—it just looked that way in English. They were actually different Chinese characters.

Nor had she anticipated having a billionaire boyfriend.

And Sierra had certainly never imagined a stranger walking up to her in a restaurant and telling her to break up with said boyfriend. The gall of that man!

She tried to redirect her thoughts yet again, but then she cut herself on the sawtooth metal strip in the aluminum foil box.

How lovely.

[5]

THE HAPPIEST PART of Sierra's week? Mornings at Moonbeam Messages before the shop opened at ten.

She got in at nine every day to prepare for opening and place orders as needed. It was her quiet time. Just her, a cup of coffee, and display racks full of cute cards and other stuff. She'd always loved stationery and gift stores. So many delightful little things that might not be considered useful but that you got for someone to show you cared.

It was the first day of the week. Well, it was Tuesday, but the shop was closed on Mondays, so it was like the beginning of the week to Sierra. She'd spent the past two nights at Colton's. To make up for missing cider with her friends, he'd bought her a necklace that she couldn't imagine ever wearing—it was just so *big*—but it was certainly beautiful. They'd watched a couple of movies in his home theater, eaten some good food, and had a long soak in his fancy bathtub.

It had been a fun weekend.

Today, Colton had some important meeting, the details of which she didn't quite understand. He had a big office in the

Financial Distract, and she had…this small store. The rent was hardly cheap, but the location was good, and she lived within walking distance.

There was an empty spot on the rack, so she went to the back to get more raccoon cards, then looked around the room before glancing down at her hand. It was still bandaged after that unfortunate incident with the aluminum foil box on Sunday. Honestly, it was a miracle she'd never needed stitches. She'd broken a bone, however—Lincoln had pushed her out of a tree when she was six, an incident she'd been blamed for, even though he'd pushed her *and* he was older.

But other than that? No visits to the ER had been needed, thank God.

She adjusted the display of washi tape, smiling at detailed plum blossoms, whimsical fairies, and gilded fans. There were also washi tape rolls with donuts and cupcakes. Dim sum. Sushi. A blue and purple watercolor background with silver stars—that was one of her favorites.

Little rolls of joy that could make someone's day.

Of course, running a store wasn't all fun and games. Profit margins were slim. Customers *weren't* always right.

But Sierra did like being her own boss, even if she had extra things to worry about. No one would yell at her for, say, taking a bathroom break once every six hours; she shuddered at the memory of her first job in retail, a lifetime ago.

It wasn't always perfect, but she'd chosen this life for herself, and overall, it was good. Colton didn't understand why she didn't dream big, why she didn't want a large chain of stores, though she didn't see why she would. One day, maybe she'd look at expanding and have another location or two in Toronto, but for now, she had her hands full.

As she sipped her coffee in the last five minutes before opening, she stared out the window at Baldwin Street. She sighed in contentment, even if the streets were slushy and gray.

Yes, this was her favorite time.

At precisely ten o'clock, she flipped the sign on the door, her sense of peace remaining as the day began in earnest.

That lasted about five minutes, until her first customer arrived.

~

It had been ten days since Jake Tong had fallen in love, an occurrence that still made zero sense to him.

However, after days spent telling himself that surely this would pass soon, he'd finally accepted that wasn't going to happen. He was irrevocably in love with a woman he barely knew.

And so he was doing something foolish.

He was going to her store.

When he entered Moonbeam Messages, it was just after ten, which he figured wouldn't be a very busy time, and he was correct. He didn't see a single person inside, not even an employee. They must be in the back room.

Much as he couldn't help longing to see Sierra, it was better this way. It would satisfy his curiosity without being too weird.

He wandered the small store. There were cards for a variety of occasions. Stickers. Washi tape. His little sister, Charlene, loved this stuff. He picked up a roll of washi tape with shooting stars and another with cupcakes.

This store was like a peek inside Sierra's mind. No doubt Colton had given her numerous ideas for how she could expand her business. Everything was about making more money and growing a business to him, but there was no trace of Colton's influence in this store, which Jake was happy to see. It looked like it was created out of love.

"Hello, could I help—Oh." Sierra jerked to a stop when she saw Jake, and the friendly smile on her face vanished. "It's *you*."

His heart beat quickly at the sight of her. Though her smile might have disappeared, he couldn't help quirking his lips. There was just something about her that drew him in, and he enjoyed the fire in her voice.

He wasn't going to walk away now.

"Yes." He held up his hands. "It's me."

"Are you stalking me?"

"No, I was just curious to see where Colton Sanders's girlfriend worked."

"And you still think I'm too good for him?"

"Yes," he said emphatically. "I do."

"So you're going to warn me away from him again?"

That wasn't the main reason Jake had come here, but since she'd brought it up...

He took a tiny step closer. "What you have to understand, Sierra, is that whatever Colton wants, he takes. He can get away with it. He has tons of people to cover up for him. So, I think there's a decent chance he's unfaithful, for starters." He paused. "Does Colton even know you at all?"

"Yes," Sierra replied, lifting her chin. "He appreciates me, unlike my family."

"Let me guess. He buys expensive jewelry that you don't wear."

She looked away, and he knew he was right, but he didn't say it.

"He understands people well in some ways," Jake said, "so he can get what he wants out of them. But that's the only reason he cares. He can make a good show of it."

"He's worked hard to get where he is."

"I'll give him that—he does work hard—but it's because he's addicted to power. To making people do what he wants. To having *more*. And he's hardly as self-made as he claims to be. You know he comes from a wealthy family, right?"

"Yes. Still, it's not like he inherited everything."

"No, but they gave him five million dollars to start his business. *Five million.*"

"You know what I think?" Sierra said, jabbing him in the chest with a single finger. "I think you're..." She trailed off, her finger still touching his chest.

Her touch almost burned him. He wanted more, and from the look of things, so did she.

He shot her a cocky grin.

"You're impossible," she muttered.

"You're still touching me," he countered.

She immediately pulled her hand back and cupped it in her other hand, as though it was injured.

"You think I'm what?" he said, taking a tiny step closer once more. "You didn't finish your thought because you were too distracted by how much you enjoyed touching me."

"Oh, for fuck's sake."

That just made him smile more.

"I think you're jealous of him," Sierra said. "That's what I think."

"Maybe I am." He looked her in the eyes as he said that. Her perfect dark brown eyes, slightly tipped up at the outside corners. "Maybe I am," he said again, softly this time. "But I'm not jealous of his money, his successful company, his private jet, or his island..."

For a moment, it was nearly silent. Just the sound of their breathing, nothing more.

"I don't need those things," Jake continued. "And I know exactly what he had to do—what many other people had to do— for him to get what he has today. It's not pretty."

"It's inevitable that you'll step on a few toes if you run a company like his."

"It's much, much more than that, and the simple fact that he was able to amass that much money—it's wrong. It shouldn't be allowed to happen. He keeps a lot of money offshore, and the small amount of tax he pays is laughable."

"Yet you worked for him."

"I did," Jake spat out, "and I regret it. Deeply."

"So, why'd you do it?"

"I was young and stupid. A middle-class kid swayed by the wealth of a friend I made in law school, who introduced me to Colton."

There was a flicker of kindness in her eyes, but then it was gone, replaced by the fire that had been there earlier.

And that was when he looked down and noticed the bandage on her hand—the one that hadn't touched him.

"What happened?" he asked.

"There was an incident with an aluminum foil container."

He reached for her injured hand, and she let him take it. Let him gently stroke it.

Yes, he was holding her hand. Caressing her skin with his thumb. And just from that, he could barely breathe. Fuck. He was a thirty-four-year-old man; he shouldn't be undone by this simple touch.

Jake yearned to close the distance between them and kiss her. Her chest was moving up and down swiftly, as if she was just as affected by their closeness as he was. He wouldn't dare go any further than this, though, even if there were a few seconds where he could have sworn she was looking at his mouth, like she was thinking about kissing him, too. But he knew she had too much integrity to actually do it, integrity that Colton fucking Sanders most certainly did not possess.

When Jake's lips twitched, she pulled back and curled her hand into a fist.

"I think you know what I want," he murmured, "but I'm not going to ask for it, not now."

"Why me?" she asked. "Because I'm his and you want to stick it to him?"

"No. The fact that you're in a relationship with my former boss is an unfortunate coincidence. I like you, and I want to get to know you better."

"You don't know me at all. You just think I'm cute."

"No, I think you're…" *The love of my life, even though it makes no sense.*

She rolled her eyes. "You can't start a sentence like that and not finish it."

"I'm not going to finish it." Jake did have some self-control.

"Very well." When she straightened, there was a mischievous spark in her eye. "I see you have some washi tape in your hand. Buy four, get the fifth free—didn't you see the sign? Seems a shame to only get two."

"They're for my sister. I really think two is sufficient and—"

"Well, I disagree." She picked up some desert sunset washi tape. "You should get this one. Hmm…and this one." The design looked like the Chinese brush painting of mountains that hung in his parents' living room. "That's four. Now, maybe something a little cutesier, since I don't know what your sister prefers. This bubble tea one, I think."

Since he figured Charlene might like that one, he didn't object. Sierra tossed him all the washi tape she'd selected.

"Okay," he said, "how about—"

"What mug do you use for your morning coffee?"

"Um, a green one?"

"Is it a unicorn mug?"

"No, but—"

"You know, I think the otter mug will suit you better." She plucked a mug off the shelf. It was actually shaped like an otter, and it looked like a pain in the ass to clean. She handed it to him before he could protest. "Any birthdays coming up?"

"Well, my brother…"

"Excellent. What does your brother like?"

"He's an environmentalist—"

"Sounds like he would appreciate this dolphin card wishing him a splashing birthday." She opened up the card to reveal an intricate dolphin pop-up, made out of different colors of paper. It was ten bucks.

Ten bucks for a greeting card!

"Too expensive for you?" she asked. "Your brother isn't worth it?"

What?

"No, I—"

"Good." She closed the card and handed it to him. "Those cards take a lot of skill. You can't just pay four dollars for them. Or do you not appreciate nice—"

"Sierra."

"Do you have any kids of your own? Nieces or nephews?"

"No, and no," he said.

"Is your mother gravely disappointed? Sorry, I shouldn't assume you have a mother… Any friends or cousins have children?"

"My friend has two little girls."

When Sierra's eyes lit up, he realized his mistake, but he couldn't back down. This was some sort of challenge—to see how much nonsense he'd put up with for her?—and he wasn't going to fail.

"How old are they?" she asked.

"Two and four."

"Perfect. They'll love this." She disappeared behind a door, and now he was very, very worried. A mug, a card, and some washi tape were one thing…

…but a giant stuffed llama was another. It was bigger than either of Quinton's girls.

"Why are you doing this?" he asked.

She shrugged. "Because I can."

"You're drunk on power."

She let out a huge laugh, and Jake started to smile but quickly forced his expression into something sterner.

"Look," he said, "my friend will kill me if I bring his girls a llama that big."

Sierra shot him a look of mock horror. With the giant stuffed animal in her arms, it was more than a little comical.

"Who are you calling a llama? This is an alpaca." She stroked the top of its head. "Sorry he hurt your feelings, baby."

Jesus.

This was both the most infuriating and the best conversation he'd ever had.

"You don't have to give it to anyone," she said. "You could keep it for yourself."

Okay, this was going a little far.

"Too much?" She gestured to a shelf containing two alpacas of a more reasonable size. One was blue and the other was green. "How about these, as a compromise? "

He leaned toward her. "You sure seem to be enjoying yourself. You like pissing me off?"

"I'm not pissing you off. I'm just doing my job. Helping you with your shopping."

Dear God, that made him want to kiss her even more.

"Fine," he said, grabbing the small alpacas. "I'll take all three."

Her expression of surprise was certainly gratifying. Her feet appeared rooted to the floor for a moment, but then she moved toward the cash register.

"Take good care of him." She patted the large alpaca's back. "He's one of a kind."

"I'm sure he is." *As are you.*

"You sound sarcastic."

"I assure you, Sierra, I'm no such thing."

"I'll ring up your purchases now. I don't think you could possibly carry any more than you already have."

He wanted to protest and lift her over his shoulder to show just how much he could carry, but that would be inappropriate.

At the counter, he pulled out his credit card.

"I don't have a large enough bag, so you'll have to carry him like that." She pointed at the giant alpaca. "And since you've been such a good customer, I'll throw in something extra for you."

"Oh, will you, now?" He raised an eyebrow.

And there she was, looking at his lips again.

He smirked.

"What the hell was that for?" she asked.

"Something extra. That sounds—"

"Dirty?"

"You're the one who said it, not me. What are you thinking about, Sierra?"

"Why do you keep using my name?"

"Because I like it. And I like you." His voice was a little rough, and a delightful shade of pink flooded her cheeks.

"You still like me?" she asked, gesturing to his purchases.

"Mm-hmm. I think I like you even more now."

"You're impossible."

He shrugged before turning to the shelf behind him and grabbing a greeting card. It had a cute illustration of two raccoons poking their heads out of a trash bin. He checked the price, slapped down a five-dollar bill—since he'd already paid for everything else—then wrote his number inside and handed it to Sierra

"If you ever need anything," he said, "call me."

"What would I need from you?"

"I dunno. Someone to carry heavy things for you, perhaps?" He hefted up the alpaca.

"That's hardly heavy. I can do it myself."

"If Colton ever does something shitty and you need to escape."

"For the last time, he treats me well."

He was certain that Colton did not treat her the way she deserved—the way Jake would treat her—but he knew better than to say such a thing now.

"Just in case," he said.

"Are you going to demand my number?"

"No. You'll contact me when you're ready."

"You seem pretty damn sure of yourself."

Well, he was pretty damn sure she was the woman for him, even if she'd made him buy out her store—maybe in part *because* of that.

But he knew he couldn't push anymore, so he would just…trust.

And act more confident than he actually was. He wasn't entirely sure what would happen, though he was encouraged by the fact that he seemed to get under her skin.

"See you around, Sierra," he said.

"Wait. I forgot to give you that something extra."

He smirked again.

She ignored it and dropped a few vinyl alpaca stickers into his bag. His gaze lingered on her hand, the one he'd stroked, and he released a shuddering breath before walking out into the sunny, cold March day.

Jake was vibrating with energy, in a way he'd never experienced before. As soon as he got home, he put away his purchases before heading to the small workshop in his basement. He was in the process of making a bookshelf for Charlene. Focusing on his work calmed him a bit, but more doubt also crept into his head.

Yes, he was in love with Sierra. Yes, he'd be better for her than Colton.

He couldn't make her do anything, though, and he wouldn't want to.

But even if she'd never be his, he needed to convince her to dump Colton's ass sooner rather than later. That jerk didn't deserve her, and he'd hate to see Colton change her into someone different. It didn't seem to have happened yet, but that didn't mean it wouldn't eventually.

Jake would know.

It had happened to him, after all.

[6]

I THINK *you know what I want.*

Those words ran through Sierra's head during her walk home at dusk. The way Jake had spoken them, so low; the way they'd seemed to settle just beneath her skin and stay there.

She shivered—and it wasn't because of the weather.

When she arrived home, Rose was sitting on the couch, watching *The Untamed*. Sierra did a double take when she noticed that Fred was also watching and had his own little bowl of popcorn.

"Hi!" Rose said. "How was your day?"

"Hi," Sierra said, sitting down in the armchair.

Rose paused the TV. "Is something wrong?"

I think you know what I want.

Those words. They just wouldn't leave. Why did they even affect her at all? Sierra had a boyfriend, and Jake *knew* she had a boyfriend.

"Got a few minutes?" she asked.

"Sure!" her housemate said brightly.

Sierra took a deep breath. "I met this guy the other weekend. He approached me and Colton when we were out for dinner, before we went to the movies. He used to work for Colton. Later, he cornered me by the washrooms and told me I'm too good for Colton. Then today, he came to the store." She swallowed. "He said he likes me. He didn't try anything"—other than touching her hand —"but I could tell he was thinking about it." Maybe that should have made her want to smack him, but instead, it had intrigued her.

Even though she had a boyfriend, whom she loved.

"And…?" Rose said.

"I convinced him to buy over a hundred dollars worth of stuff at the store, including the big alpaca I keep in the back."

"You sold Big Freddy?" Rose ate a handful of popcorn from Little Freddy's bowl.

"I'm sorry," Sierra said. "Were you saving up for him?"

"No." Rose paused. "So you're in a love triangle. Having never been in a love triangle before, I don't have any advice to offer."

"Oh, I don't need *advice*."

"Are you concerned about him? Like, he won't leave you alone and he'll follow you home?" Rose leaned forward.

"No, I don't see him doing that. He didn't ask for my number. Gave me his number, though, saying I'd contact him when I was ready."

"Sounds a little arrogant. What does he do now, if he doesn't work for Colton?"

"No idea. Anyway, I'm just venting because he annoys me." *And I can't get his words—or the warmth of his thumb stroking my hand—out of my brain.*

Rose nodded, looking more somber than usual. Sierra was about to ask if something was up when Rose's phone rang.

Rose looked down and picked it up right away, which meant it must be her father. She always answered when her father called, and they talked several times a week, whereas Sierra couldn't imagine having a conversation that lasted more than three minutes with her own dad.

She headed to the kitchen to make herself some dinner and spent the rest of the evening trying her very best to keep Jake out of her brain.

Unfortunately, she failed in a rather spectacular fashion.

But her fixation didn't mean anything was actually wrong with her relationship with Colton, right? It was just a little blip. That annoying man and his intense gaze were stuck in her head like a kid's song that your nephew insisted on listening to over and over and over again.

It was nothing more. She was certain of it.

"So," Quinton said, sipping his coffee. "Explain the llamas?" He gestured at his two little girls, who were playing an incomprehensible game with their new toys.

"Alpacas," Jake mumbled as he set his mug on the end table in Quinton's living room.

A mug that was *not* shaped like an otter, unlike the one he'd used at breakfast.

"What's the difference?" Quinton asked. "I mean, I know they're different animals, but in stuffed animal form, when one is blue and the other is green? How was I supposed to know they're alpacas rather than llamas?"

"I don't know." Jake stared at the toys in question. "But that's what she said they were."

"She?"

"I met someone."

"Yeah?" Quinton's face broke into a grin, his teeth bright against his dark brown skin. "That's great."

"She owns a card and gift store. She, uh, made me buy a bunch of things, including..." Jake pulled out his phone and showed his friend a picture.

Quinton put on his glasses. "Is that a giant llama—sorry, alpaca? On your bed?"

"It is."

Quinton slapped his knee and laughed.

"What's so funny, Daddy?" asked Liv, the older of the two girls. She spoke in a very serious voice—she took after her mother more than her father, at least in temperament.

"Jake just told me a funny story. I'll tell you later. At bedtime."

To Jake's surprise, Liv was satisfied with this, and she returned to her toys.

"I've got eight hours to think of a story," Quinton said. "I should be able to manage."

"She won't forget?" Jake asked.

"Liv never forgets. The other day, I was wrapping a birthday present for Melody, and Liv said it was the same wrapping paper I used for her birthday last year. I pulled up the pictures, and sure enough, she was right. But back to your new woman."

Jake and Quinton had been friends since law school. Quinton had gone on to work in family law, and Jake…well. There'd been a few years when they hadn't seen much of each other, but they hung out regularly now, when Quinton's schedule allowed. He was the one with a full-time job, a wife, and two kids, whereas Jake didn't have any of those things.

"Did she agree to go on a date with you after you bought not one, not two, but three stuffed alpacas from her?" Quinton asked, laughing again.

"No. And she's not single. She's in a relationship with Colton Sanders."

Quinton almost spilled his coffee. "You're shi—" He glanced at his daughters. "I mean, you're kidding me."

"No."

"Let me get this straight. It's been a long time since you've been interested like this in a woman, correct?"

"Yes."

"Like, a long, *long* time. Since law school."

Jake glared at his friend. "Could you get to the point?"

"And this woman's dating Colton Sanders?"

"I already said that."

"Colton Sanders is actually in the relationship?"

"Apparently."

"Liv, don't steal your sister's alpaca. You have your own." When Liv obeyed—for now, at least—Quinton smoothly returned his attention to Jake. "Where did you meet this woman?"

"I saw her at a restaurant and told her that Colton's no good for her."

"I'm guessing she didn't want to hear it. Did she tell you to stay away from her?"

"No. Then again, she never suggested she'd be open to the idea of seeing me again."

Some of her body language had told another story, though— and that's why Jake couldn't help but hope. Did she have that kind of sexual tension with Colton? If not now, then at the beginning?

Somehow, Jake couldn't help thinking that she hadn't.

"I gave her my number when I was at her store," Jake said. "Told her to call me if she ever needed anything."

"And now you're going to wait until she calls?"

"Well…"

"Jake," Quinton said, serious now, "you have to leave this alone. She made a decision. She's in a relationship with Colton, like it or not—actually, *is* that the only reason you want her? Because you want to take something from him, and it's impossible to hurt him financially."

"No," Jake scoffed. "I wanted her before I saw she was with Colton."

He'd have no qualms about hurting Colton. If it was against the bro code because Colton had once been his employer and friend, Jake didn't fucking care.

But it was true. Sierra had made a decision.

For now.

"Don't do anything stupid," Quinton said.

Yes, Quinton was right, and Jake should take no for an answer.

That was one of the differences between him and Colton, after all. Colton Sanders didn't accept "no." He threw his money and influence at something until he got what he wanted. Perseverance was one thing, but sometimes refusing to listen to other people's feelings and opinions was just entitlement.

Jake had given Sierra his number. He'd bought three alpacas, among other things, from her store—which he hoped showed that he was serious.

The ball was in her court.

Jake wasn't a romantic comedy fan, but as he walked home from Quinton's—a long walk, but it was a nice day—he desperately thought of all the rom-coms that Charlene had watched back when they'd both lived at home. She'd played those movies over and over. Going to them for hope and inspiration felt like a new low, but he needed something.

He recalled one movie in which two people, both in relationships with others, met over the last pair of cashmere gloves at a store. They chose to let fate decide whether they should meet again. The woman wrote her number in a book and gave it to a used bookstore, and the man wrote his number on a five-dollar bill.

This had seemed truly ridiculous to Jake back in the day, and it seemed ridiculous to him now. He didn't believe in fate.

But the fact that he'd met Sierra in the restaurant...that felt like fate.

Hmm.

By the time he got home, his head was a bit of a mess, but

then he got a text from an old friend who'd bought a table for a charity gala and wondered if Jake wanted a seat.

Jake normally would have said no, trying to stay as far away from his old life as he could. These days, he volunteered at the food bank once a week rather than attending glitzy benefits. But Colton would probably be there, which meant there was a decent chance that Sierra would accompany him.

It was a big event, and Jake wouldn't try to talk to her, but if she approached him, well…

He'd try to help fate along, just a little.

[7]

"Oh *wow*," Amy said as Sierra came down the stairs.

Amy and Rose were sitting on the couch in the living room. Amy was visiting from next door for this special occasion of watching Sierra get dressed up for a charity gala. Since she and Colton had been keeping their relationship a secret, she hadn't attended larger events with him before, but tonight, she'd be seen on his arm.

She did love her gown. It was long and red and actually made her look like she had boobs. She hadn't been allowed to see how much it had cost. She also wore the big necklace that Colton had bought her, and even the crystals in her hair were probably worth more than her rent.

The hair stylist and makeup artist—provided by Colton, of course—followed her down the stairs. They, too, had done an excellent job.

She felt like Julia Roberts wearing that red dress at the opera in *Pretty Woman*.

But although Sierra knew she looked stunning, she also felt a bit uncomfortable. She wasn't used to wearing such clothes.

Would she trip over her feet and destroy a tray of champagne flutes? Given her luck, it seemed rather likely.

"'Wow' is right," Rose said. "You look amazing."

A few minutes later, a limousine pulled up. Colton got out to meet Sierra as she came down the steps in her silver shoes.

Truly, it was like something out of a modern fairy tale, so why couldn't she fully enjoy the moment? Was it just the fear that she'd do something silly or clumsy? Her mom's voice at the back of her head, telling her that she wasn't meeting expectations?

"You look incredible." Colton made a show of kissing her hand and helping her into the limo—she was now used to riding in limos.

"You're not so bad yourself," she said lightly.

Indeed, he looked quite handsome in his tux.

On the drive, he tried to kiss her, but she was afraid of messing up her makeup, though perhaps the fancy makeup artist had used a special type of lipstick that never, ever smudged.

"I'm nervous," she admitted. "I'm not used to these sorts of events."

"Don't worry," he said. "I'll be by your side the entire time, and you know I'm a pro." He winked at her, and she felt somewhat reassured.

Standing at one of the high-top tables in the ballroom, Jake downed his posh wine and looked around. Expensive décor. Rich men who didn't give two shits about how they treated their workers but made a big splash at exclusive fundraisers.

Christ. He hated the reminder of who he used to be and swore he'd never be again.

His gaze landed on Martin Dunham, his former close friend. When they'd met in undergrad, Jake had been impressed with the wealth of the Dunham family. Martin had invited him to a "cottage" in the Muskokas, a cottage that was more of a palace to Jake. Martin had made him feel like he was special and could accomplish anything, maybe have a similar place of his own one day.

Nobody had believed in him like that before.

Jake now knew that was unfair to his family. Sure, he'd sometimes felt overlooked as the middle child, who wasn't a whiz kid like his older brother, but Mom and Dad were good parents. They'd valued him for who he was and cared about integrity. Unlike the Dunhams, for example, who were just obsessed with capitalism.

Martin Dunham had set Jake on the path that had led him to Colton Sanders.

"Martin," Jake said.

The other man ignored Jake's coldness; he was all friendly smiles. "Still working for Colton Sanders?" It was surprising he wasn't up-to-date.

"No, got a little project of my own."

Martin probably envisioned something very different from the truth. They chatted for a few minutes before Martin was, thankfully, distracted by someone more important than Jake.

Maybe coming here had been a mistake. He should leave before dinner and—

That was when he saw her.

Sierra arrived on Colton's arm, but Jake's attention was all on her. She was wearing a red dress, and although there were many beautiful and well-dressed people in this room, there was still no one like her. She was utterly incandescent.

He knew then, with absolute certainty, that he'd never find another woman more beautiful. It was impossible.

She tilted her head up to whisper something to Colton. Colton nodded before turning his attention away from her. He'd just gotten here, and he was already ignoring his date.

Jake didn't understand. Not at all. If he'd arrived with Sierra, he'd be by her side all night, then whisk her away before midnight to…

He didn't let himself finish his thought, and he didn't let himself approach her.

She hadn't seen him yet, and maybe she wouldn't.

Sierra was annoyed.

Colton had promised to remain next to her. He knew an event like this would make her uncomfortable. Nearly everyone here was a stranger to her, and she found the idea of approaching these strangers rather intimidating.

That woman's tiara must be worth as much as my home! And I can't even afford to buy the house I live in.

She didn't belong here.

True, she was also wearing expensive jewelry and a gown from some exclusive designer, but she felt like a fraud. Like it was false advertising.

Yes, she'd been dating Colton Sanders for over a year, but for much of that time, she'd begged him to keep it quiet, not wanting to tell her family yet—and also afraid that other people would tear her apart if they knew. Because she obviously didn't belong with someone like him.

Now that he'd walked away, she felt as if she'd been thrown to the wolves.

Were people looking at her funny, or was that her imagination? Were they whispering about her, saying she must be a shallow social climber? Did they think she was too plain for a man like Colton, even though she knew she looked good tonight?

And although Toronto was a diverse city, the crowd at this particular gala seemed very, very white. Perhaps that was why she noticed Jake Tong. He was one of the few Asian guys in the room.

What the hell was he doing here?

Except he fit in more than she did, didn't he? He'd been part of Colton's inner circle—she had no idea what he did now—and that tux looked like it was made just for him.

For a split second, she wondered if he were here because he wanted to see her again. Her heart beat embarrassingly quickly at the thought.

She shook her head and told herself she was being silly.

And then he turned in her direction. Her mouth parted in an "O," and she couldn't look away. No matter how much she willed herself to look in the opposite direction, it wasn't happening. She was transfixed by his gaze. The heat, the intensity of it.

That didn't make sense. There must be at least twenty meters between them; it wasn't like they were close enough that he could lean forward and kiss her…

Why the hell was she thinking of kissing him?

The corners of his lips tipped up in an infuriating grin, as though he knew exactly what she was thinking about.

Sierra grabbed a glass of wine off a tray and drank it faster than she ought to.

Shit. Now she was light-headed. She snagged a smoked salmon something-or-other, which helped a bit, but she needed fresh air. She hurried toward the doors at the far end of the room, nearly tripping in her new shoes, and sighed in relief when she was outside.

Yes, this was better. Much better.

The fancy venue was located on the waterfront. She stared out at the dark lake as she took deep breaths and—

"Hey."

The voice startled her. It was quiet and not as low as Colton's…because it didn't belong to Colton Sanders, but Jake Tong.

Out here, in the night, he looked different. The shadows over his face made him more mysterious. Dangerous. He was holding out his jacket, and that, too, seemed like a dangerous gesture.

She shook her head. "I don't need it."

"You have goose bumps on your arms."

Did she? She hadn't noticed.

"It's March," he said. "It's hardly warm out here."

"Won't you be cold?"

"Don't worry about me."

She shouldn't take his jacket. It seemed wrong. But now that he mentioned it, yes, she was a little chilly. Had she not noticed because of the adrenaline coursing through her veins?

When she nodded, he draped the jacket over her shoulders, and she was acutely aware of how close he was. She nearly leaned back against him to capture some of his warmth, but he stepped away.

"Are you feeling okay?" he asked.

"I'm okay now. Too many people inside." She pulled the jacket tightly around her. It smelled nice.

"Are you usually like this in crowds?"

"Never, but I'm rarely in crowds like this one."

"Where's Colton?"

She shrugged. "I don't want to bother him. Not his problem."

"You're his girlfriend."

"I'm sure he has important business."

"You're important."

The sincerity in his voice was startling. Frightening. She pulled his jacket even tighter as armor, but that didn't work as intended because it was *his* jacket.

"That's one of the things Colton likes about me," she said defensively. "I'm low drama. Undemanding."

"It's fine to have some needs. Don't make yourself small just to fit in someone else's life. You know, I wouldn't..." He shook his head and looked out at the lake.

"You wouldn't what?"

He shook his head again.

It was somehow very important that he finish that sentence.

"Jake," she said.

Finally, he turned toward her, his gaze dipping below her face. There was a cool gust of wind off the lake, but his perusal of her body made her flush.

"If you were my date," he said, his eyes meeting hers, "I wouldn't abandon you."

"That's what he said, too."

"But I'd actually follow through."

The wind was wreaking havoc on her hairdo, but she didn't head inside. She was rooted to the ground.

She believed him.

But she'd been with Colton for a while, and they had a good relationship. She shouldn't throw anything away just because some man she barely knew was sweet-talking her.

"You look beautiful tonight," Jake said. "In case no one has told you."

"My friends did. Colton did, too."

Yet none of their words had affected her as much as the guy standing before her now.

"He's not a bad person," she said, perhaps more to convince herself than Jake, but she didn't dwell on that. Besides, she was used to having to defend her choices. It was second nature. "He donates tons of money."

"I know. He makes a big deal of it, so people know exactly how good of a 'philanthropist' he is. But at the same time, he keeps doing damage, and nothing negates that. His donations don't change a broken system; Colton *is* the system. He likes it that way. Nothing is ever enough for him."

Nothing is ever enough. She was reminded of what she'd asked Colton on the night she'd met Jake.

But she felt like being contrary because she resented how Jake made her feel.

"You think Colton provides me with nothing but a little money and glitz," she said, "but you're wrong. I feel way more appreciated with him than I ever do in my own family."

"That's a travesty. You deserve better."

"How can you say that when you hardly know me?"

"I feel like I know you well, even if we've only met a few times. I can't explain it."

Under his jacket, goose bumps were breaking out on her skin again. Good thing he couldn't see them.

"You think a woman who forced you to buy a life-sized alpaca—"

"I object to it being called 'life-sized,'" he said. "It wasn't *that* big."

"It's at least the size of a baby alpaca. Therefore, life-sized. Where do you keep it?"

"In my bedroom."

Now she was having unwelcome, inappropriate thoughts about his bedroom. This man was certainly pissing her off.

"As I was saying," she continued, "you think a woman like me deserves more than a boyfriend like Colton Sanders? You think I'm a paragon of virtue?"

"Who said you were a paragon of virtue? I don't think that, but I do like you a lot."

"Jake, did you come tonight because of me?"

"I wasn't positive you'd be here, though it may have crossed my mind."

"But it was part of the reason you came?" she pressed.

The seconds before he answered were some of the longest in her life.

"Yes," he said.

She'd thought she was foolish earlier, yet here he was. Confirming that he'd come here partly for her.

It shouldn't send a thrill through her body. She was happy with Colton, dammit. He could be thoughtful, and he'd arranged for her to have this beautiful dress and hair and makeup that made her feel like a queen.

Well, she felt more like someone who didn't belong here pretending to be a queen, but still. She looked great. Jake thought she looked great.

More importantly, so did Colton.

"You have to stop doing this," Sierra said.

"Doing what?" Jake asked.

"Showing up in my life. Don't come to my store again."

"Alright. I won't."

She was disappointed at his words, but she shouldn't be. He'd just said he'd do exactly what she wanted.

"I wasn't going to talk to you tonight," he said quietly, "but then you looked disoriented and stumbled out to the balcony alone."

"So, you were watching me."

"I wasn't following your every move, but my eye was drawn to you because..." He gestured toward her. "It's hard to avoid looking at the most gorgeous person in the room."

If anyone else had said that, Sierra would have rolled her eyes, but she didn't feel the urge to do that now, maybe because it felt like Jake had spoken with utter sincerity.

Still, she made a joke of it. "Even with your jacket covering me up?"

"I like seeing you in my jacket."

He'd probably also like seeing her in one of his dress shirts, with only a button or two done up...

When she heard a noise behind her, she turned. Colton was striding toward her.

"Sierra," he said, ignoring Jake. "What are you doing out here?"

"I was feeling a little light-headed, and I don't know many

people, so I was just talking to Jake." Really, that was all they'd been doing. Talking.

Colton removed the jacket from her shoulders, handed it back to Jake without looking at him, then placed his own jacket around her. It was different from how he'd acted around Jake at the restaurant—did he see Jake as a threat now?—but she couldn't think about that any further.

"Let's go inside, darling," Colton said. "Or I can have someone take you home if you're not well." He looked at her with concern.

See, Jake? He cares about me.

"I'll be fine," she said. "I feel better after a few minutes outside."

"I'm glad."

In truth, she felt better in some ways, but she also felt like she was on a seesaw.

He led her back inside, and she exchanged a glance with Jake over her shoulder. She wondered if she'd see him again. She hoped she didn't, yet at the same time…

Colton was attentive for the rest of the evening and introduced her to lots of people. He left her side for ten minutes to talk to someone, but that was all.

They posed for pictures. He kissed her cheek.

She choked down some food that she ought to appreciate.

Afterward, they went back to his place and collapsed into bed. Well, Sierra collapsed, but Colton still had a bit of energy. He kissed his way up her neck and made a show of stripping off his formal clothes.

"Not tonight," she said as he held himself above her.

"Mmm. Tomorrow morning, then. You know, I was thinking…why don't we go away in a couple of weeks, just the two of us. I still haven't taken you to my island. Ask Marisol to work some extra days at the store."

"She can only work weekends."

Still, Sierra was warming up to the idea. She rarely shut down

Moonbeam Messages, and she hadn't been on holiday in a long time. Plus, she couldn't deny that she was curious about his island in the Caribbean.

"Sounds good," she said. "Let's do it."

She was excited about this…wasn't she?

[8]

THE NEXT DAY, Jake took his frustration out on wood. He'd finished Charlene's bookshelf and was now working on two bedside tables. She'd recently gotten an apartment with her boyfriend of three years, and they'd bought their bedside tables from IKEA and screwed up the assembly. When Charlene had given him the tour of her new apartment, those bedside tables had offended him, so he'd decided to make his little sister something better.

It wasn't like he got many commissions. It was more of a hobby that made him a little money than an actual job—and that was fine for now, though he should think more about what to do with his life. He didn't have a mortgage, and his bank account was healthy enough. That was what being one of Colton's top guys had done for him.

It was nice to make something tangible. Feel the wood beneath his fingers.

Jake took a break to sip the dregs of coffee in his otter mug. He hadn't been able to sleep last night. He'd been replaying his conversation with Sierra over and over again. The way they'd looked at each other as she'd headed back inside with Colton.

Goddammit. He was jealous of that jerk, and it had nothing to do with the man's wealth.

But was Jake really much better than Colton?

He wanted someone else's girlfriend. He'd gone to her store. He'd stood with her alone in the night. The fact that he was in love with Sierra—was that just a sign that he wasn't as good of a man as he thought?

He'd dedicated the past two years to improving himself. To being someone who could actually look at himself in the mirror every morning without shame.

Except he could barely do that now.

He pictured Sierra in that red dress...in his bedroom. He'd press a kiss to her neck as he unzipped her. The dress would pool at her feet, and she'd shoot him a seductive smile over her shoulder because she was his and didn't need to deny her attraction. He'd pull her tight against him, show her just how hard she made him as he kissed her mouth. She'd beg him to touch her. Beg him to give it to her good.

Fuck, why did the thought of her begging get him so worked up?

He needed some self-control.

Jake gave his head a shake, turned on the sander, and lost himself in his work and self-loathing until it was time to go to Mississauga to see his family for lunch.

Mom had wanted something "different" for lunch today, so they were at a Szechuan restaurant rather than one of their usual places. Mom, Dad, Lewis, Victoria, and Charlene. Charlene's boyfriend wasn't here because he was at work.

"Are you around next weekend?" Jake asked Charlene as he helped himself to the mapo tofu. "I'll have your bookshelf and tables ready by then. I can drive them over."

"That would be great. Thank you so much. You're the best big brother."

Lewis made a quiet sound of protest.

"You know that soon enough Jake will do something to get on my nerves," Charlene said, "and you'll take his place again. Don't worry." She patted Lewis's shoulder.

Charlene was always playful, even with people who were the opposite of her. She won everyone over eventually.

"How's the job search?" Dad asked.

Jake pretended he didn't know who his father was talking to and helped himself to the green beans. Perhaps he should try harder to earn his father's respect. Dad valued hard work above everything else.

"Jake?" Dad prompted.

"He doesn't need a job yet," Mom said. "Jake, you have enough money, don't you?"

"Because he worked for that asshole whose workers don't get proper breaks," Lewis bit out. "Did you hear how many suffered from heat stroke?"

"Can we please try to have a nice dinner?" Mom said. "Put aside our differences?"

"People are being mistreated."

"Wait, which workers are these?" Charlene asked. "I've never heard of this."

"It was in the paper last month," Dad grunted.

"I'm sure it's an exaggeration," Mom said soothingly.

The green beans didn't taste as good as they ought to.

"It's not," Jake said. "He was trying to diversify, so he bought—"

"I don't think this is appropriate lunch conversation."

"Then let's talk about how he polluted—" Lewis began.

"I'm not arguing. Not anymore." Jake held up his hands. "Colton does lots of bad things and gets away with it, I agree. When he gets bad press, it doesn't hurt him much. It's not fair.

Nobody should be able to amass that much wealth, but we've been through this a hundred times before, and I don't work for him now."

"But you still socialize with him, apparently."

"What are you talking about?"

Lewis reached for his phone. "Someone posted a picture of you two at a gala last night."

It was a picture on the balcony. Sierra was just visible in the background, Jake and Colton in the foreground.

"You look constipated," Charlene said.

"Thanks," Jake replied dryly.

"No, you two look friendly," Lewis said.

Mom frowned. "Those are very different things."

Dad looked at the picture. "Jake looks the same as he always does."

"Yeah, he doesn't have a wide range of expressions," Charlene said. "Only a small difference between constipated and friendly for him."

"Who's the woman in the background?" Victoria asked. "Wait, is that the woman we saw at the restaurant last month? The one you were talking to?"

Damn Victoria and her great memory.

"It's Sierra," Jake said. "Colton's girlfriend."

"He has a girlfriend?" Charlene asked.

"Aiyah!" Mom said. "I'm tired of hearing about this man. He's tearing apart our family. For the rest of lunch, we won't talk about him."

The table was quiet for an uncomfortably long time.

"So," Victoria said at last, turning to Charlene, "how's your new apartment?"

Because Jake lacked self-preservation, he looked at photos from the gala on social media the next day. He usually avoided social media because it was a hellhole and probably bad for his blood pressure, but here he was. On Twitter.

Though he hadn't posted anything in two years, he still had his account. He was tempted to reply to some of the nonsense he saw, but managed to restrain himself. A few of the tweets were fine, but a lot of them...

Colton Sanders is dating a nobody?

Is she some heiress from China?

Apparently her name is Sierra Wu. Like the movie.

It was a book first, you dumbass.

She's nothing special.

This is why being an Asian guy sucks. All our women ignore us and date guys like this.

How'd she land a guy like him? She must have great skills, if you know what I mean...

Jake was seething by the time he saw a link to a sketchy dating site, which was aimed at white men who wanted a younger, submissive Asian woman.

Not that he hadn't thought about taking off Sierra's red dress himself, but he wasn't posting shit online. He was keeping his inappropriate thoughts on another man's girlfriend in his own brain, thank you very much. Nor was he fetishizing her in some weird way, though he suspected that was part of the reason Colton was with her, based on his experiences with Colton at strip clubs—and lots of other places.

He wished he didn't know this stuff, but he did.

A week later, Jake went to Kensington Market to pick something up, and since he was in the area, he figured he'd walk by Moonbeam Messages. Not that he'd go in, of course; Sierra didn't want that, and he'd respect her wishes, but he thought there was no harm in walking by.

He stopped in front of the store. There were cards in the window for Mother's Day, which was coming up next month, but curiously, the store was closed, even though he'd have thought it would be open at this time.

Then he saw the sign on the door, stating that she was on vacation and they'd be open on Saturday.

He had to restrain himself from clenching his hands into fists. She was almost certainly on vacation with Colton, maybe at that ridiculous island he owned.

Jake couldn't help feeling more than a little jealous, and he was just cocky enough to think that Sierra would have a better holiday if she were with *him*. He remembered the energy that had crackled between them, and he kept wanting, wanting, wanting.

Wanting what he couldn't have or shouldn't have.

Story of his life.

He caught a glimpse of his reflection in the window and curled his lips in disgust before hurrying down the sidewalk.

[9]

ALTHOUGH SIERRA HAD REGULARLY BEEN EXPOSED to luxury in the past year—private jets, penthouse suites at European hotels, and necklaces worth more than the average house in Toronto—she still wasn't quite prepared for Colton's private island in the Caribbean.

"Is that a *hotel* on your island?" she asked as the plane descended.

"It's an exclusive resort, only open twelve weeks a year," Colton said. "The waitlist is long, and it doesn't come cheap."

She hadn't realized this island was a commercial enterprise; she'd thought it was just his private getaway.

No, she hadn't Googled it. She'd wanted to be surprised.

And it was breathtaking. As they approached, she could see that three-quarters of the island was in its natural state. The colors were vivid, and as they disembarked from the plane, the heat hit her skin. She closed her eyes and sighed in bliss. The weather was warming up in Toronto, but it was still nothing like this.

They headed to what Colton called his "cabin," aka a mansion.

It had a courtyard with tropical flowers and a terrace overlooking the ocean. Lots of glass walls to enjoy the stunning view.

One small thing she'd read about the island, when she'd Googled Colton a while back, was how he'd come to buy it three years ago. He'd been out on a billionaire friend's superyacht, noticed this oasis of green in the distance, asked if it was for sale, and the rest was history.

He pulled Sierra against him in the courtyard. "I'm glad you're here with me. You know, you're the first woman I've brought here."

"Am I?" She giggled when he kissed her neck.

Sierra spent the next hour exploring and marveling at a random assortment of things. The cell service and Wi-Fi. (How much would that have cost to set up?) The umbrellas on the terrace. (Yes, she loved a nice umbrella.) The waterfall in the distance. (A small waterfall, but still. He had his own private waterfall!) The collection of beachwear in her size. (Which was a little weird, to be honest, and none of the stuff was cheap.)

"So, you do like it?" he asked, and to her surprise, he didn't sound as cocky as usual. He sounded a little...unsure.

"Of course I do," she said.

Later that afternoon, they drank cocktails on the beach and went on a short walk to the waterfall. Sierra had a great time, but she also felt a little guilty. It was just too lavish. She didn't need this.

Colton's attention was on her the whole time. He wasn't taking calls or checking emails or figuring out how to make as much profit as possible.

He was simply hers.

That evening, they had dinner on the terrace and watched the sun set over the ocean. It was just the two of them—and the person serving their multi-course meal. Sierra wore a simple yet elegant wrap dress that she'd found in the closet, and her hair was loose, fluttering in the warm breeze. Colton sat across from her, his sleeves rolled up to his elbows.

She catalogued all the perfect details about this scene, starting with the wine and food. The first course was conch salad, which she'd never had before. It was delicious.

Before the next course, Colton leaned forward and took her hands in his. "You're very special to me."

She hated that this was the most romantic moment in her life and she wasn't a hundred percent into it. What was wrong with her? The setting was unbeatable, but something felt off.

Was Jake getting into her head?

She tried to focus on the man in front of her. Countless women would kill to be in this position.

"When you're like me," Colton said, "it's hard to know who truly likes you, and who pretends to like you because of your connections and money. Or because they want to stay at the resort on your island."

"I can imagine."

"But those aren't the reasons you're with me."

No, I'm with you to impress my family.

She put her hand over her mouth, even though she hadn't spoken.

"Is something wrong?" he asked, concern in his expression.

"Nope, not at all." She was just disturbed by the thought that had popped into her mind.

She wasn't with Colton only to impress her family, right? Why, she hadn't even mentioned him until recently. Sure, she'd relished the shock and awe on her mother's face, but that was merely a side benefit of being with him.

"It's hard for me to trust people," he continued. "But I trust you, Sierra. I used to struggle to imagine myself in a relationship. Then I met you, and you changed me. You don't expect and demand luxury…"

Wait. Did he think all the other women he'd known were gold diggers?

"You just want a little of my time," he said. "You're fiercely independent—and incredibly sexy, of course."

She imagined telling Sierra-from-three-years-ago that when she was thirty-four, she'd be dating a wealthy man who brought her to his private island and arranged a lovely dinner outside at sunset...and she imagined telling Sierra-from-three-years-ago that such a thing wasn't all it was cracked up to be.

When the server returned with plates of crab, Sierra immediately dug in.

Colton watched her. "I like that you enjoy your food unselfconsciously and aren't worried about every calorie. And you're not afraid to occasionally call me out on my shit. You're a good influence on me... Why are you laughing?"

Oh. She was laughing, wasn't she.

She was trying to imagine Ma saying she was a good influence on someone, and her imagination failed her. Sierra had always been told to be more like Rachel or Grace, rather than being liked for who she was.

But Colton didn't say such things.

"Thank you," she said. "That means a lot to me."

She studied him for a moment. Those blue eyes. That chiseled jaw.

He was a sharp businessman. He knew how to persuade people to give him what he wanted. Was he being honest, or just telling her what he knew she wanted to hear?

But she had no wealth or properties that he was after. If he wanted sex, it wasn't like he needed to be in a relationship with *her* for that. Before they'd started dating, he'd had a reputation for being a playboy; if she left him—not that she was thinking of leaving him, was she?—there would be a lineup of women ready to take her place. A few women had given her dirty looks at the gala.

No, she trusted him like he said he trusted her...right?

Later that night, she snuggled up to Colton and wondered why his body had to be so damn hard and uncomfortable. Not that she didn't appreciate the way he looked; she just wished he was a little cuddlier.

But he was a human, not a stuffed alpaca. It would be silly to compare the two.

Then she found herself comparing Colton to Justin, her ex-husband, and she didn't like this train of thought, but she couldn't seem to help it.

Yep, there was definitely something wrong with Sierra, as Ma never failed to remind her.

And with that cheery, familiar thought in her mind, she drifted off to sleep.

The next morning, they watched a K-drama.

Colton, to Sierra's surprise, had expressed an interest in K-dramas. She suspected this wasn't purely for entertainment, but because K-dramas were popular and he had business aspirations related to them somehow...

Or maybe she was being unkind.

They were partway through the second episode of *Romance is a Bonus Book* when her phone rang. She took a quick look at the display. Her mother.

She'd ignore it for now, but there was a good chance that her mother would call back.

She turned the sound off, and sure enough, her phone vibrated a minute later.

Sierra was having a lazy morning in bed with her boyfriend, watching TV on his giant screen. She put a pillow on top of his chest and rested her head on that. It wasn't how she'd expected to spend the morning in a tropical paradise, but it was a good way to pass the time, something that would not be true of talking to her mother.

When her phone started vibrating again, she said, "Sorry, I should really take this," to Colton and headed out to the terrace.

"What's up, Ma?" she asked with a sigh.

"You finally picked up the phone! I thought you were dead, and I didn't even know which country you were in."

"How did you know I was away?" Sierra didn't share details of her life with her mother when she could help it. If she was going away for less than a week, it wasn't worth the hassle.

"I walked by Moonbeam Messages and that's what it said on the sign. You tell any stranger who passes your store, and you don't even tell your own mother you're on vacation?"

"You actually walked past my store?"

"I thought I'd pay my daughter a surprise visit. You foiled my plans!"

Yeah, that was Sierra, always doing the wrong thing.

"I'm away with Colton for a few days," she said. "That's all."

"Where are you? Mexico? Jamaica? His private island?"

"Yes, actually."

Ma shrieked. "You should have invited us."

And this is why I didn't tell you.

"It's his island," Sierra said, "not mine."

"We'll go some other time. You should be wooing him with your charms. Maybe he took you there to propose." Ma gasped. "Did he propose and you're not telling me because you like to keep secrets from your poor mother?"

"No, he didn't. I'm hanging up now."

Rather than listening to ten minutes of protest from Ma, Sierra ended the call right away.

She needed a minute to compose herself, so she looked at Fred's Instagram. Rose had joked about stowing Fred in Sierra's luggage so he could travel the world and have his picture taken on Colton's private island—a place where no alpaca had gone before—but in the end, Fred had stayed in Toronto. From the look of things, he'd spent some time reading.

Sierra went inside, climbed into bed, and rested her head on Colton's pillow-covered chest.

"Everything okay?" he asked.

"Yeah. Conversations with my mom are always overwhelming, that's all."

He chuckled and wrapped his arm around her before restarting the show. The heroine's life was a bit of a mess, so Sierra could relate.

A few minutes later, Colton pointed at the screen. "She's pretty cute."

After a beat, Sierra said, "This is where you tell me that you've seen better." She wiggled against him.

He laughed. "You're right. She's cute, but not as cute as you."

"I like him. Lee Jong-suk."

"Really?"

"Why not? He's a model, you know."

"He's too pretty," Colton said.

Sierra started to worry this conversation would go in places she didn't want it to go—did Colton fail to understand how anyone could be attracted to Asian men?—so she playfully walked her fingers up his arm. "And this is where I tell *you* that I've seen better."

They watched another two episodes, and that afternoon they spent time on the beach, followed by another romantic dinner on the terrace.

"Mmm," Sierra said as she polished off her seafood stew. "The chef is amazing."

"He is."

She smiled at the server as he whisked their bowls away. When he was gone, she looked back at Colton. "I hope you're paying the staff well."

"Of course," he replied, though he looked stiff for a moment.

Possibly her imagination.

"Give them a nice bonus when we leave." She'd never said something like that to him before, but if she was dating a billionaire, she could tell him how to spend a very small amount of his money, couldn't she?

After a decadent dessert with chocolate and coconut, he gave her a white gold hairpin with a dizzying number of diamonds. It was beautiful, but not at all her style. A year ago, she wouldn't have cared about that; the fact that he'd gotten her such a gift would have been enough to make her feel special.

But now...

That night, she had a fitful sleep. She dreamed that Colton was having phone sex with another woman while Sierra was right next to him, but when she woke up, of course he wasn't doing anything of the sort. He was fast asleep, the blankets pushed down to his hips, and when she looked at him, she felt...nothing.

People would kill to be in your position, Sierra. Don't forget that.

She walked onto the terrace and looked out at the ocean. It was so incredibly beautiful.

That was why silent tears trailed down her cheeks, right? Because she was overcome with the beauty of it all?

No, she had to stop lying to herself.

She was crying because she'd realized just how much Colton didn't understand who she was as a person. She didn't truly love him—how could you truly love someone who didn't see you?— yet she'd stayed with him because he made her feel like she was someone who mattered. But given what her family was like, the bar for that was super low.

Being out of Toronto, out of her regular life, had made those things clearer, and seeing his personal island had also made her even more uncomfortable with his wealth. She had to stop burying her head in the sand. Stop being blissfully ignorant of how Colton got his money.

Sierra took out her phone and pulled up an article about how shockingly little he paid in taxes. She'd heard something to that effect before, but she'd never actually seen the numbers.

Then she found an article about workers wearing diapers at a warehouse he owned, not for medical reasons but because they weren't given bathroom breaks.

She hadn't even known he owned this company.

She found yet another article, this one talking about how Colton had built his business from nothing, i.e., with five million dollars from his family, as Jake had stated.

"Hey, baby."

Sierra startled as Colton came up behind her.

"Can't sleep?" he asked, wrapping his arms around her.

"Uh, yeah. Can't sleep." Did she sound guilty? Should she feel guilty simply for Googling? She was just looking at articles that anyone could find.

"You like it here?"

"It's lovely."

"I don't know why I took so long to bring you here. We should come more often. I'll give you the money to hire another employee for your store—"

"I'll think about it." She didn't feel like talking about this right now.

He kissed her temple and slid his hand down her body.

"I'll come back to bed soon," she told him.

A moment later, she was alone again, looking out at the dark ocean, the waves lapping the shore down below. She closed her eyes and imagined Jake's arms around her, his lips pressing a single kiss to her neck.

She shivered, which she hadn't done when Colton had kissed her—and he'd actually been here, whereas she was just imagining Jake.

Jake, what are you doing to me?

[10]

"So?" Nicole leaned forward. "How was it?"

Sierra sipped her cider. "What are you referring to?"

Nicole gave her a look. "Your trip with Colton. What else?"

Right. That. It seemed so long ago, even though she'd only come back last week.

Now, after a day at the shop, she was out with her friends at Ossington Cider Bar. Colton would be joining them shortly. He'd promised he'd come today and wouldn't be distracted by business.

She believed him. Mostly.

"It was beautiful," Sierra said, injecting some pep into her voice. "Even more so than I expected. Private dinners at sunset by the ocean, and there was even a waterfall."

"Sounds romantic." Amy sighed dreamily.

"It was," Sierra said.

Nicole looked a bit skeptical. "You enjoyed yourself?"

"Of course!"

There was a pause, as if everyone was waiting for Sierra to add more, but she didn't.

Yes, these were her closest friends, and they'd been there

when her marriage had gone out with a whimper. Aside from Amy, whom Sierra hadn't met until more recently.

Yet she couldn't tell them the truth. Couldn't tell them that she hadn't loved the trip as much as she should have, that she'd considered breaking up with Colton. But upon returning to Toronto, some of her doubts had eased. Perhaps the excitement was gone simply because they'd been together for a while. It was only natural, right?

Fortunately, the conversation moved on to other things.

"We finally found an apartment," Charlotte said.

"That's wonderful. Where is it?" Nicole asked.

"In the building next to Mike's. Literally right next to it. After months of looking…but this one wasn't available when we started." Charlotte gulped some cider. "I can't wait to begin packing."

"No sarcasm detected there." Nicole laughed. "Nope, none whatsoever."

"I mean, I *am* happy about it. It's just a lot of work. How's David?"

"David's fine, except exams are coming up and he'll have lots of marking to do."

"I'm sure you'll make sure he takes frequent breaks," Sierra said.

"Don't worry, I will." Nicole smiled as she pulled out her phone.

After finishing her first cider, Sierra went to the washroom, and when she returned, Colton was in her seat.

Her first instinct was to say something snarky like *so glad you could grace us with your presence*, but she kept it to herself and pulled up another chair. Then she leaned forward and greeted him with a kiss on the cheek.

When she sat back in her chair, she could have sworn Nicole was giving her an odd look.

"So, uh, Colton," Nicole said. "Own any other islands?"

"I have a few," he said smoothly.

"Yeah, he owns like two thousand islands in the Thousand Islands," Sierra quipped.

"No, just three or four."

"Wait, you *do* have islands in the St. Lawrence River?"

"Yep."

"See," Charlotte said, "there are always new things to learn about each other in a long-term relationship. I should ask Mike if he secretly owns any islands."

"You really don't have to be rich to own one," Colton said. "There are islands that cost less than half a million bucks. I saw one just last week on—"

"Is there a special website for buying islands?" Sierra asked.

"There is."

Huh. There was so much she didn't know.

"I imagine some islands do go for pretty cheap," Charlotte said. "Islands that are now underwater much of the time thanks to climate change, for example. Maybe Mike could afford one of those."

"Maybe," Nicole murmured.

There were several seconds of awkward silence.

Hmm. Conversation wasn't flowing as usual, as if Colton's presence—and he was fully present and not distracted by his phone—was throwing everything off. Or maybe it was only Sierra's imagination and she was just cranky today.

At eleven o'clock, they got ready to leave the bar.

"You know what I could go for?" Rose asked. "Late-night dumplings."

"Oh my God, yes," Nicole said. "Too bad there's nothing around here."

"Actually," Colton said, "I know a place. Very close."

Charlotte and Nicole looked skeptically at each other, as if to say, *This white guy probably doesn't know what he's talking about.*

But Sierra couldn't deny she was curious to know what Colton had in mind.

And when Amy said, "Sounds good to me!" they all followed Colton.

To Sierra's surprise, Colton led them to a rundown Chinese dumpling shop on Dundas. Huh. She hadn't known this was here, at the edge of Little Portugal. Though it was close to the cider bar, she rarely ventured west of Ossington when she was in the area.

It had all the things she looked for in a dumpling shop: it was clearly all about the food, because it sure wasn't about the appearance. It also seemed like it had been around for a while.

Colton knowing about such a place was more unexpected than him owning multiple islands in the St. Lawrence, and it was surprising he wanted to eat here.

She wondered how he'd heard about it.

After spending a few hours at a bar with Quinton and other friends from law school (only half of whom were still lawyers), Jake started walking to the subway station. But then he was inexplicably pulled to the south, toward the dumpling place he used to frequent back when he'd lived in this area.

Okay, that wasn't really inexplicable. It was perfectly sensible to want dumplings after a few beers, and they were open until midnight. He still had time.

When he arrived ten minutes later, he looked at the sign for a moment, trying to remember the last time he'd come here.

The owner—a man slightly older than Jake's father—greeted him, clearly remembering him even if he hadn't been here in a while. Jake would have said a few more words, but he was distracted. Not by the delicious smell of dumplings but by that laugh.

Sierra.

The seating area wasn't large, and it didn't take long to locate her, sitting at a table with several other people. Four other women he didn't know—her friends?

And Colton Sanders.

Jake walked over to the table. "Hi, Colton. Sierra."

Sierra didn't say anything, but she wore a guilty expression.

Interesting.

He hoped she'd been having the sorts of thoughts about him that he'd been having about her. Naked in the shower thoughts and such. He'd sworn that he wouldn't seek her out again, that his feelings for her were wrong, but this had been unplanned.

Maybe he did believe in fate after all.

"Jake," Colton said. Even the sound of his voice made Jake want to punch the man's skull. "Good to see you."

"Come, uh, join us," Sierra said, as though she wasn't sure this was a good idea.

Jake pulled up a chair to the end of the table. The group already had their dumplings.

"I'll order my own food, don't worry," he said. One of Sierra's friends passed him a menu, but he already knew what he was having. C5.

Once he'd ordered, Sierra introduced him to the other women.

"How do you and Sierra know each other?" the woman named Nicole asked.

"Colton and I go way back," Jake said. "In fact, I was the one who first took him to this restaurant." He had a feeling that going here had been Colton's idea, and he didn't want Colton getting all the credit.

"How's Big Freddy?" Rose asked before picking up a dumpling.

Sierra looked at her in alarm.

Jake was confused. "Who's Big Freddy?"

"The giant stuffed alpaca you bought at her store," Rose explained.

Ah. He hadn't realized his alpaca had a name.

His lips twitched at the puzzled look on Colton's face…and at the fact that Sierra had apparently told her friend about him. That was a good sign.

"He's well," Jake said, then tried to shoot lasers out of his eyes at Colton.

Alas, he failed.

His dumplings arrived, piping hot, and he dug in, careful not to burn his mouth. However, Sierra soon drew his attention away from the taste of his wonderful pork and chive dumplings. She was lifting a dumpling to her mouth with her chopsticks, and his attention zeroed in on her parted lips.

He shifted in his chair and tried, once again, to shoot something, anything, at Colton. Lasers, glitter, knives, some combination of the above.

This was torture.

"Sierra and I spent a few days at Sanders Getaway recently," Colton said.

"Oh. Yes. It was beautiful," Sierra stammered.

Colton had picked up on Jake's interest and was now bragging about his private island, which Jake had been to more than once. The asshole had also named the development on the island after himself.

Probably Colton was trying to say, *You can't touch her. You're not in my league. You don't even have your own island.*

No, Jake did not, but he had things like compassion and morals.

But he had to accept that Sierra was still with Colton.

Jake hated, absolutely *hated*, the thought of Sierra on vacation with Colton. In bed together. Having lunch on the terrace.

Colton's lips curved in the tiniest smirk, which Jake didn't think anyone else noticed. But he'd spent a lot of time with Colton, and he recognized that smirk. He'd seen it in boardrooms on several occasions.

He didn't like being on the receiving end of it.

He couldn't leave immediately, though. That would be too much of a win for Colton. Besides, Jake still had three dumplings left.

After finishing them in a hurry, he made his excuses, something about being an old man and needing to get home to bed. Words were coming out of his mouth, but his mouth wasn't connected to his brain right now.

He just knew he needed to get out.

Outside on the sidewalk, he leaned over and put his hands on his knees like he was recovering from a run, even though he wasn't winded.

"Hey."

He jerked his head up. Sierra was standing in front of him.

"You okay?" she asked.

"Yeah," he said. "Why?"

"You don't look okay."

I'm in love with you and I can't stand seeing you with him.

He didn't say those words, of course, even if his brain and mouth weren't fully connected, but he thought them, and he felt like she understood them, too.

She reached for his hand and squeezed it before withdrawing. There was a touch of sorrow in her eyes, but she hadn't changed her mind.

He held himself back from kissing her, instead turning and walking toward Bloor. It felt like her eyes were on him the whole way, even though it was more than a kilometer.

He took the subway home and got ready for bed, and before he switched off the light, he looked at Big Freddy keeping watch in the corner of the room.

Sierra had told her friend about Jake. She'd run out of the restaurant without a coat to talk to him again.

He fell asleep with a faint smile on his face.

~

The next morning, however, was a different matter.

Jake cut himself shaving because he was barely able to look at himself in the mirror.

When he squeezed his eyes shut, his mind wandered to Sierra taking that dumpling between her lips, and this, naturally, led to thoughts of her doing other things with her mouth.

Now he was getting hard. For fuck's sake.

He should not be thinking about her like this—he shouldn't be thinking about her at all, but especially not on her knees for him.

It was crude. Inappropriate.

She was Colton's girlfriend. Who cared if she'd come out to talk to him last night? That didn't matter.

Jake braced his hands on the bathroom counter and willed his brain and body into submission, but it didn't last long. He couldn't stop himself from shedding his boxers and stroking his dick. The thought of her lips around his cock was impossible to resist. He tried concocting a different face in his imagination, but it was hers. It had to be hers.

He furiously jerked himself off, needing to get this over with as quickly as possible. He imagined sliding into the wet heat of her pussy as she squirmed and begged him to take her…

Jake came in his hand and leaned against the counter, disgusted with himself.

And as he cleaned himself up and prepared to face the day, he imagined holding her afterward and pressing tender kisses to her neck.

Dammit.

He was trying to be a better person, and these feelings weren't part of his plans.

[11]

"WHAT'S UP?" Sierra asked.

Something was up. She could feel it. Nicole hadn't invited her here simply because she wanted to have congee, though Sierra definitely approved of the restaurant. She hadn't been to this Chinatown hole-in-the-wall in a long time, and the congee with thousand-year egg and pork was excellent.

Her friend looked overdressed for the restaurant. Nicole had come straight from work, and she was wearing a skirt suit. Sierra had also gone into work today—the store wasn't open, but she'd had things to do—and was wearing something much less fancy.

Nicole set down her spoon. "Sometimes, Colton looks at me funny. The first time, I thought it could be my imagination, but it's definitely not."

The warm food couldn't stop the chill that traveled through Sierra's body. "W-what do you mean?" she asked, even though she was pretty sure she knew.

"Like he's checking me out, especially my breasts. Like he's thinking about how I look underneath..." Nicole gestured to her top.

Sierra's first instinct was to deny it and defend her boyfriend.

But why should she defend him? Nicole would never lie about this. It sounded like she was only telling Sierra because it had happened multiple times, and she wouldn't have said anything if she wasn't sure.

"He creeps me out a little," Nicole said.

"I'm sorry." Sierra's delicious congee had lost its appeal.

"You can do better than a man who checks out your friends and rarely shows up when he says he will."

Sierra's instinct was to argue with that as well. *How can I do better?*

But instead she said, "I'm really sorry. He shouldn't have…" And then she blurted out, "Jake said I deserve better, too."

"Jake? The guy we ran into at the dumpling place?"

"Yeah. He used to work for Colton. Hates him now."

"I did sense that." Nicole paused. "I can't deny it was an interesting conversation, however brief it was." She raised her eyebrows, as if hoping Sierra would add more.

Sierra picked at her food, like she was a white person who thought congee could be improved by the addition of raspberries, chocolate bars, or similar. Her emotions were a tangle, and Colton was away for more than a week.

Which was a relief, actually.

"Hi, Gung Gung," Sierra said cheerily, but her heart was sinking. She could already tell he wasn't having a good day.

He nodded at her but didn't speak as she took a seat beside him. Thanks to transit issues, she was the last to arrive for dim sum.

"How is your boyfriend?" Ma asked after they'd placed their order.

"He's fine." Sierra didn't want to talk about this, but she wasn't surprised that was her mother's first question.

"You still haven't shown me pictures of your island vacation."

"Oh, right." Sierra pulled up the photos on her phone and passed it over. "Have a look."

"Why don't you sound more enthusiastic? Are you already bored by all his wealth? Unimpressed by diamonds and rubies and… Ah, look at that house! The view! You must marry this man. Why does your bathing suit have so much fabric?"

"You think I should have been topless all week? And taken pictures of it?"

Po Po looked disgusted by the turn in conversation, which was *not* Sierra's fault. Ma had started it.

"I'm just saying," Ma said.

"It's my life. Let me handle it."

"Aiyah! Why should I do that? You're so bad at handling it."

"Gee, thanks."

"Ah, this is all very interesting, but you must see the nice dress Rachel got for me." Auntie Marlene pulled out her phone. Clearly, she was tired of the conversation revolving around Sierra.

Sierra wasn't sure she'd ever been so glad to hear her aunt brag about Rachel.

"You know how many hours she worked last week?" Auntie Marlene asked. "Seventy! But she still found time to get this for me and to look after her kids and house."

Sierra was exhausted just thinking about it. Poor Rachel should be at home sleeping rather than being subjected to this nonsense.

Yes, there was good food—ooh, the siu mai had arrived—but as Sierra studied her cousin, Rachel's mask seemed to slip, and she looked as exhausted as she ought to feel.

"Rachel," Auntie Marlene said, "show us the nice couch you're thinking of buying."

"Later," Rachel murmured. She was helping her children with their food while her husband loaded up his own plate.

"Lincoln," Po Po said, and everyone else shut up. "How are you doing at work?"

Sierra's brother looked pleased that people were finally focusing on him—as though he didn't already get enough attention. He was Po Po's favorite, presumably because he was the only grandson. Auntie Marlene had two daughters; Rachel's sister was out in Vancouver and didn't need to endure these family get-togethers.

Perhaps Sierra should move to the other side of the country, but she liked Toronto, and her friends were here. Plus, moving was expensive.

"I got another promotion," Lincoln said a little smugly.

Sierra rolled her eyes. Lincoln was forever announcing promotions at family meals. She knew they were lies, but he got away with it because no one questioned him like they questioned her.

"Sierra!" Ma snapped. "Be happy for your brother."

Sierra was so not in the mood for this.

She also wasn't in the mood to argue. Too much energy.

"It's impressive that you get so many promotions," Ma said to Lincoln.

"It is," Rachel said. "It's impressively...suspicious." She daintily picked up a piece of bao with her chopsticks.

Sierra managed not to guffaw. Was perfect Rachel really...?

"What's your title?" Rachel asked.

"Senior engineer," Lincoln said.

"And what was your title before?"

Lincoln hesitated. "Senior engineer."

"Did you get a raise?"

Ma sniffed. "It's impolite to talk about money like that."

Sierra couldn't hold in her laugh now. Her mother was saying it was impolite to talk about money, as if she didn't do that all the freaking time?

"Sierra," Ma snapped again.

"Okay, no money talk," Rachel said. "What are your new responsibilities, Lincoln?"

"Well, I'm on a new project—"

"Ah!" Rachel said, as if this had clarified everything. "Thank you for explaining. I understand now. When you say 'promotion,' which you say at least six times a year, you mean you got a new project at work. But there are always new projects, right?"

Sierra wanted to high-five her cousin.

"Rachel," Ma admonished.

Auntie Marlene, on the other hand, beamed at her daughter, while Po Po looked at everyone disapprovingly.

Sierra helped Gung Gung reach an egg tart as yelling erupted around them.

"Thank you," he said. "You will visit me soon?"

Po Po and Gung Gung lived in a Chinese retirement home with memory care services. It was better for everyone involved than them living with either of their daughters. Also, Ma and Auntie Marlene got to brag about being able to afford it.

"You can bring your husband," Gung Gung said. "I have not seen him in a while."

"Okay, Gung Gung."

"And bring something from your store for me, yes?"

Sierra smiled. He did remember her store. "I will."

She snuck him another egg tart. No one was paying attention to them, so no one would complain that it had too much saturated fat, sugar, or similar. She also poured more tea for him. Not too much, though—his hand was shaking more than usual on the cup, and she didn't want any tea to slosh over the top.

"It's still a promotion!" Ma shouted. "Your daughter was nit-picking."

"Your son was lying," Auntie Marlene shot back, "and your daughter is also a liar. You think she's actually dating a billionaire? Ha!"

Even in this loud, chaotic dim sum restaurant, they were starting to cause a scene.

On the plus side, it prevented Sierra from thinking too much about what was happening with Colton, although she was insulted that Auntie Marlene thought she was lying.

Or maybe her aunt didn't think that but was just saying shit in the heat of the moment. Who knew. The heat of the moment was, like, half the time her family was together.

The argument finally ended when Lincoln's baby let out the loudest shriek that Sierra had ever heard in her life—it was truly impressive—and Lincoln shoved the baby into his wife's lap and ran to the washroom.

"Your son can't take care of his own children!" Auntie Marlene shouted.

"He's my son, not my daughter," Ma said. "He shouldn't have to take care of babies."

Okay, Sierra had been wrong about the argument being over.

Come on, Ma. It's the twenty-first century.

"Are you fucking kidding me?" Rachel actually raised her voice. "Will you two cut it out?"

Well, this was it.

The family had finally broken Rachel.

It was just before ten, and Sierra had finished stocking the shelves. She sipped her coffee as she looked outside at the pouring rain.

April showers bring May flowers.

She hoped something good would come to her life soon.

Her family was in tatters and she'd stopped picking up the phone when her mother called.

Her boyfriend was checking out her friend and talking about traveling to space. No, he didn't want to train to be an astronaut;

there were now companies that specialized in space travel for rich people. It was another world—literally—to Sierra, and she didn't approve. Couldn't the money that a billionaire spent going to space be used to lift hundreds of people out of poverty? Clean up the lake that his company had polluted?

The bizarre conversation about space travel had taken place via text. Colton was in Europe for a couple of weeks, and Sierra wanted to wait until he was back to have a serious talk. A voice in her head, which sounded suspiciously like her mother, told her that she shouldn't do anything rash.

It wasn't like Colton was cheating on her, after all, although Jake had suggested that was a distinct possibility.

How can a woman like me even keep a man like Colton Sanders?

But he could have continued his previous lifestyle if he'd wanted; instead, he was in a relationship with her.

Usually, this was Sierra's favorite time of day. Her coffee, her empty shop. But her insides had been a swirling mess for over a week, and the rain was coming down hard.

April showers bring May flowers.

But what would today bring to Sierra Wu?

$$[\ 12\ ]$$

THE FEMALE CHARACTER shot the hero a look that was painfully like the one Sierra had given Jake on Saturday, on the sidewalk outside the dumpling shop. There was zero resemblance between the actress and Sierra, but something about that look…

Jake shut off his TV but stayed on the couch, his elbows on his knees.

She was still with Colton, who'd taken her to the island where he never took women. Yet even though she'd recently come back from a trip to paradise, Sierra had seemed rather sad on Saturday night.

Colton likely hadn't noticed, but Jake had noticed it, dammit.

She wasn't happy.

Before he knew what he was doing, he'd put on his shoes and was out the door. He needed to hurry if he was going to get there in time.

The subway train came mercifully fast—any minute of waiting would be agony to him—and it wasn't long before he was in Baldwin Village.

He *had* to see her.

At a minute to six, he approached Moonbeam Messages and

put his hand on the door, breathing a little hard because he'd been sprinting.

He looked through the door, and Sierra stared back at him. Her hand was on the "open" sign, about to flip it to "closed."

But she'd stopped mid-motion.

She wasn't wearing anything special. Just a pink long-sleeved T-shirt under her blue apron. Jeans. Hair in a haphazard bun, a few strands loose around her ears.

She was fucking beautiful.

At last, he snapped himself out of his trance and opened the door.

"Are you still open?" he asked quietly.

"Yes."

"Good."

And with that, he flipped the sign, locked the door, and pulled down the blinds.

"What are you doing?" She moved behind the counter, as though it were safer there.

"I'm not buying anything today."

"I didn't ask you to. In fact, I told you not to come back to the store."

"I stayed away for more than a month, but I can't do it any longer."

"Why not?" she asked.

"Because I want you too badly."

"You want me because I'm with him, and you hate him."

"It's not like that," Jake said. "It's not like that at all."

She was breathing heavily, too, her nostrils flaring, and why did he find that cute?

"Tell me this." He leaned forward across the counter. "How was your trip to his tropical paradise? Have the time of your life?"

"It was fun." Her lips trembled as she said it.

"Not all you hoped it would be, was it? You wished you were there with me instead of him, didn't you?"

She gripped the counter. "You're a fucking arrogant jerk, you know that?"

He couldn't help chuckling. "Only where you're concerned."

"I don't think that's true."

He shrugged. "Get to know me better and see what you think."

"How do you propose I do that?"

"Start by breaking up with him."

"Jake—"

"What would you do if I kissed you now?"

She looked away, which made him smile.

"I wouldn't kiss you, of course," he said. "I know you wouldn't appreciate it because you're still with *him*." He practically spat the last word. "But you want it, don't you? You hate that you want me, but you do. You've imagined being in my arms, my lips on yours…"

"Why would I think of such a thing?" But there was no anger behind her words.

She'd definitely thought about it.

His lips quirked up, and he grabbed a stuffed panda off a shelf. "If you're telling the truth, then swear on the life of this panda. 'I, Sierra Wu, have never thought of kissing you, Jake Tong.'"

"You," she said, "are a ridiculous man."

"But I could be *your* ridiculous man." He shook the panda then set it on the counter. "Maybe something else will have more of an impact. A unicorn?"

He was about to step toward the shelf of stuffed animals when he felt her hand on his. He immediately turned back to her, but he didn't say anything. She was touching him and his brain had short-circuited or blasted into outer space or…something. He ached to touch more of her.

"Stop this nonsense," she said before letting go of Jake.

His heart was still hammering. "Why is it nonsense? You're

with him, but you don't have to be. I can give you many things that he can't."

"Like what?"

"Time, for example, which I'd spend getting to know you better than anyone else does."

"What if you don't like what you find?" she asked.

"I'm not worried."

"Why not? Seems only sensible to be worried about that."

He shrugged. "Somehow, I just know."

"Wow, great logical reasoning there."

"I'll make you things with my own two hands," he said, "rather than paying someone to do it for me. Dinners, tables, whatever you like."

"There's a big difference between a dinner and a table."

"And I can do both. I'll also meet your parents, which I bet Colton hasn't done."

"Now I'm certain you're a ridiculous man," she said. "Any reasonable person would have to be dragged kicking and screaming to meet my family."

"Maybe I'm not fully *reasonable* now, but I'd still do it. For you."

"Stop telling me these things. We're not together. As you are very, *very* well aware, I'm dating someone else, and this is entirely inappropriate."

He had a smart-mouthed comeback, but he didn't say it.

She was right. He'd painted himself as the one who had actual morals, unlike Colton, and here he was, telling a woman who was already in a relationship that she should be with *him* instead.

He'd felt compelled to hurry to her store, but he hadn't stopped to think about what he was doing. When he'd walked out of Colton Sanders's life, he'd vowed to be a better man—and now he was failing at it. Miserably.

"Okay," Jake said softly.

"Please don't come here again. I mean it."

He nodded.

"Say it," she snapped.

"I promise not to come here again. For real, this time."

He pushed himself away from the counter and headed out the door, not looking back.

He walked down Baldwin Street slowly, shoving his hands in his pockets so he didn't literally punch himself in the face. He hated that he'd come here, though he still wanted her, his morals be damned. He couldn't help wanting her.

When he got home, he grabbed his gym bag and went to the gym. He worked out longer than usual, punishing his body. Hoping that if he pushed himself hard enough, it would push her out of his brain. Out of his heart.

He needed to get over her.

Sierra slid to the floor in Moonbeam Messages and leaned her head against the wall.

Was she really any better than Colton, who'd checked out her friend's boobs?

She was lusting after his former friend. Not just a *Yeah, he's handsome*, like she might say about Lee Jong-suk. She'd even touched Jake's hand for a moment too long.

In fact, she found the whole thing a little…romantic.

It seemed wrong. He'd gone against her wishes and come to the store.

But she couldn't help it. His inability to stay away from her was hot, even though it shouldn't be.

She closed up the store and walked home, not able to pay full attention to her surroundings. She nearly stepped in front of a bike, and afterward, she was so shaken that she had to wait a full minute before she could continue.

At home, Rose was sitting on the couch, scrolling through Netflix.

"You'll never guess what happened today," Sierra said as she took a seat.

Rose focused her attention on Sierra, but when Sierra opened her mouth, she realized she couldn't tell her roommate everything. Couldn't say how hot and bothered Jake had made her feel. What would Rose think of her?

"Jake came to the store," Sierra said carefully. "He told me…he couldn't stay away. He told me the things he could give me that Colton can't and…" She trailed off at the look on Rose's face. She hadn't said anything about her own feelings, but Rose already appeared to be judging.

Then she saw the tears in Rose's eyes.

"I'm sorry," Rose said. "I can't listen to you talk about how you have *two* men interested in you. It's not enough that you have a super rich boyfriend who takes you to his private island."

Sierra wished everyone would shut up about the island.

"But you have a second guy desperate to be with you," Rose continued, "and I…" She looked down. "I have no one. I haven't dated in ages. I know I shouldn't resent you for it—you're my friend—but…"

"Rose." Sierra moved to hug her, but Rose stood up and turned off the TV.

"And please don't give me platitudes. I've heard them all before. I'm tired of people telling me that I'm such a sweet person and the right man must be out there somewhere. It doesn't change the fact that I'm alone. You, Nicole, Amy, and Charlotte all have someone, but not me. Nicole didn't even want a relationship, and now she has one, and he's perfect. I just…I can't…" Rose hurried up the stairs, and Sierra knew better than to follow when Rose wanted to be alone.

She'd given Rose such platitudes in the past, it was true. Because she believed them. Clung to them because she didn't want to live in a world where such things didn't happen. Rose, more than any of them, was the romantic, even if she didn't talk about it much. She deserved to find love.

Sierra made herself some noodles for dinner, feeling even guiltier than she had before.

[13]

Sunday morning, Jake woke up hard, thoughts of Sierra filling his brain. That apron she'd worn yesterday, on the floor…his hand sliding into her jeans, finding her so wet for him…her gasp as he slipped a finger inside her….

He reached for his dick and stroked himself a few times before cursing.

He'd sworn he wouldn't do this anymore.

Jake forced himself out of bed, put on his running gear, and headed outside. He pushed himself to go twice as far as usual, like he was training for a damn half-marathon.

But, just like yesterday, exhaustion didn't do the trick.

When he returned, after running farther than he'd ever run before, he was aching and dripping with sweat, but he still yearned for her.

Goddammit.

What he needed was to get away. Out of the city, to a place where he hadn't been since last fall.

His cabin.

~

Look outside.

When Sierra received that text from Colton, she leapt to her feet and looked out her bedroom window.

There was a white limo on the street, and Colton was sticking his head out, waving at her with a bunch of red roses. The neighbors' dog—a white ball of fluff named Beast—was barking up a storm at the scene, and Sierra couldn't help smiling.

But there was a pit of dread in her stomach.

It was Friday. She wasn't supposed to see Colton until tomorrow evening. She'd been working up the courage to talk to him about Nicole, as well as the stuff she'd read about him. Some of the things she'd found out about his business dealings were more than a little alarming.

Be down in five, she texted him.

She quickly changed into something more befitting of a ride in a limo: a summer dress and cardigan with hoop earrings, rather than cut-off shorts and a tank top. Truthfully, she was somewhat annoyed that she had to put on proper clothes. After checking her hair in the mirror, she hurried downstairs.

Colton stepped out of the limo to greet her with a kiss on the cheek. "You look lovely."

"You're not too bad yourself," she said.

But inside, she was thinking, *Shouldn't I be more excited to spend time with my boyfriend? I haven't seen him in more than a week.*

Maybe it had something to do with all the money he kept offshore to avoid paying taxes.

Or the rumored poor working conditions at a meat processing plant, which was part of a company he'd inherited from his maternal grandparents. (How had she never known about that?)

Or the union busting.

Or the shoddy construction at his latest resort and the possibly underhanded tactics he'd used to buy land.

Yet despite her mess of feelings, she was still delighted when she stepped inside the vehicle and found champagne and a charcuterie board. She loved charcuterie boards.

"This looks awesome." She grabbed a piece of prosciutto. "Where are we going?"

"This is all I have planned. Thought we'd just drive around for a while."

She'd told herself before that Colton didn't know her at all, but she'd been wrong. He knew she wouldn't be in the mood to go to a fancy restaurant or bar, so instead they were having a quiet evening, driving around in a limo with a shitload of delicious meat and cheese and crackers.

He kissed her on the lips before pouring them each a small glass of champagne, and she took a healthy swallow as complicated emotions warred within her.

"Are you okay?" There was concern in his eyes. He really was thoughtful.

She wasn't prepared for the conversation she ought to have with Colton, so she curled up against him instead. She was a mess, but he cared for her.

For today, she'd enjoy this ride in a limo. This luxury.

And then tomorrow, they would talk.

When Sierra woke up in Colton's bed the following morning, bright light was streaming through the windows. She hadn't set the alarm on her phone, and she had to open the store in half an hour.

"Shit, shit, shit," she muttered as she got dressed.

No one said anything in response.

Because Colton wasn't in the room with her.

That didn't matter right now. She had to get to Moonbeam Messages. She hurried through the ginormous house, and before she reached the front door, Colton's assistant called to her.

"Colton had to rush off to an emergency business meeting in Calgary," Weston said. "He sends his regrets"—that sounded like he was declining an invitation to a party he didn't want to attend—"and asked me to ensure you get to wherever you need to go. He'll be away for a few days."

Relief washed over Sierra. She knew she was a scaredy-cat, but at least she wouldn't need to have any difficult conversations with Colton tonight. They could wait a little longer.

"Thank you," she said.

Weston handed her a coffee, for which she was grateful. "Did you enjoy your charcuterie board yesterday?" he asked.

"I did."

He smiled. "I picked it out when Colton said he wasn't in the mood to be seen in public but wanted to meet up with you away from home."

That put last night in a different perspective. *Of course* Colton hadn't picked out the food himself, and *of course* the plans had been all about him, not Sierra; the two things just happened to align.

Traffic was light, and she made it to Moonbeam Messages in good time. She thanked the driver and headed into her store, where she took a few minutes to prepare for the day. For some reason, it felt like she'd had four double espressos rather than a single caffeinated beverage.

It was the last day of April, and she had no idea what May would bring.

I should have said something to him last week.

That was what Sierra thought to herself as she flung herself into an Uber on Friday after work. Usually, she took transit everywhere, but she wasn't in the mood today, and Colton's house near the Bridle Path was rather awkward to get to by public transit. People who lived in houses like that didn't take the TTC, though the people who worked for them might.

Colton had come back from his mysterious business trip on Wednesday, and they'd made plans to see each other tomorrow for dinner, but Sierra couldn't wait any longer. This was weighing on her mind, and she needed to talk to him.

Yet as the Uber made its way north, she heard her mother's voice in her head.

He looked at Nicole's boobs? Who cares! He's only a man. He can't help himself. And her boobs are hard to miss...

Ma didn't like Nicole, whom she'd met on a couple of occasions, including Sierra's wedding. She disapproved of how Nicole dressed and didn't like that Nicole's mom's family were Toisanese peasants who'd come to Canada with nothing. Apparently, Nicole's good job didn't make up for that. Ma also didn't like Charlotte, whom she thought had a "bad attitude."

You will never do better than Colton Sanders. Wah, I don't know what he sees in you!

Sierra shoved that voice away. Her mother made her feel shitty enough with her actual words; she wouldn't let Ma's imaginary words hurt her, too.

The Uber dropped her off at the gates to Colton's house. Yes, his house had fucking gates. She entered the security code, which changed every month, then walked up the semi-circular driveway.

Normally, she'd head to the front door, but she stopped before she reached it. There was a limo in the driveway, which was a little odd. Not *that* odd, but she frowned. There was noise coming from inside, and before she could think about what she was doing, she opened the limo door.

It took her a moment to process the scene in front of her. There was just so much skin.

Colton Sanders, *the* Colton Sanders, was half-naked in a limo with two other women.

[14]

Jake was driving back into the city. Spending five days at his cabin had done him good. Being in nature had revitalized him and made him feel less out of control. Less like the man who'd run to Sierra's shop in a fit of desperation.

He'd bought the cabin after getting his first bonus from Colton, and Colton had assumed the structure would be torn down for something larger. The fool that Jake had been six years ago had actually considered it, but even then, only briefly.

No, it was good exactly how it was.

He hadn't been able to stop himself from fantasizing about having Sierra there with him. Drinking morning coffee out of cheap mugs on the porch, then going back to bed for a few hours...

But the thoughts hadn't consumed him as much as they had before.

Though when he plodded up the stairs to his bedroom and saw Big Freddy, something clenched inside him.

He wouldn't go to her again. Instead, he'd throw himself into some yard work.

Yep, that was a great way to spend a Friday evening.

~

Although Sierra had thought she might break up with Colton tonight, this certainly wasn't what she'd had in mind.

Two women were naked and licking his cock. Both of them were Asian, and somehow, that made everything worse.

Which was perhaps why the first words out of her mouth were, "Are we all fucking interchangeable to you?"

She'd never actually thought about what she'd do if she caught her boyfriend cheating. But if she had, she probably would have imagined shouting words like, *You bastard!*

She added that now for good measure.

"You bastard!"

She felt like an idiot. Colton fucking Sanders just had a weird thing for petite Asian girls, and he'd probably only bothered with her because of her name. *Sierra Wu.* It must have been amusing to date a woman with the same name as a demon slayer, that was all.

She'd made a horrible, horrible mistake.

"I can explain," he said, but the two women were still touching him, and he didn't bother getting up.

"You going to say it's not what it looks like?" Sierra asked. "Don't bother. We're over."

She shut the door to the limo before he could reply and hurried down the ridiculous driveway and out the ridiculous gate. Then she pulled the creased raccoon greeting card out of her purse—yes, she'd kept it. She entered the number written inside, practically stabbing the phone with her fingers.

"Hi," said a familiar voice.

Thank God he'd picked up. She didn't know what she would have done otherwise.

"It's Sierra," she said.

"Is something wrong?" Jake asked.

Yeah, she probably didn't sound too happy right now. Only

reasonable: her boyfriend had been cheating on her with not one woman…but two.

That she knew of.

What had he been doing for the past year and a half? He could have been sleeping with half the damn city, and she was the sucker who believed he wouldn't cheat. Were all of his "business trips" really business trips?

Sierra shouldn't have been so damn naïve.

But Colton Sanders had swept her off her feet just by paying her a little attention and not saying she was a failure. And buying her fancy things—often not to her taste—that cost such a small percentage of his wealth; it would be the equivalent of her buying a candy bar, if that.

She shouldn't be so angry at herself. He was the one who'd cheated, not her.

And to think she'd felt guilty for experiencing mere sexual tension with another man, when Colton was literally fucking other people!

"What happened?" Jake sounded concerned at her long silence. "Do you need me to come get you?"

"Are you at home? Are you alone?"

"Yes—"

"What's your address?"

He told her.

"Okay," she said, "I'll be there soon."

She ended the call before he could say anything more.

Jake paced his hallway.

He'd desperately wanted Sierra to call him, but not like that. No, his fantasies had been more like, *Hi Jake, I broke up with Colton because I realized you're the one I love after all.*

Instead, she'd been furious. Not at him, but someone had hurt her. She'd practically barked out the words.

He'd been trying his best to move on, but he wouldn't turn her down when she needed him. Whatever she asked for, he would give it to her. He would make things right.

There was a knock on the door, and he opened it right away.

"I caught him cheating on me," she spat out. "His dick was in someone else's mouth."

Jesus.

"That fucker," Jake muttered.

"You gonna gloat?"

"*What?*"

"You did warn me."

"But I never wanted that to happen." He paused. "Why are you here?"

She jerked backward. "Fine. I'll go."

"No." Jake was messing this up. He put a hand on her shoulder. "Just wondering why you came to me rather than getting drunk with your friends. Do you want me to beat him up?"

She let out a mirthless chuckle. "I don't want you to get in trouble."

"Then what..." He lost his ability to form words when she trailed her finger down his chest. His throat was suddenly as dry as the tundra, and her outfit—heels, jeans, and an off-the shoulder red shirt with short sleeves—sure didn't help.

"I want you to help me forget," she said.

Oh, fuck.

He had to be absolutely sure of what she meant. He pulled her into the house and shut the door behind him. When he stepped close, he cupped her cheek in his hand.

"Like this?" he whispered.

"Yes."

She'd barely finished saying the word before he crushed her against his chest and kissed her with everything he had, unable to wait for a second longer. He'd wanted her since the moment he first saw her.

And now, he didn't have to hold back.

He hated that his asshole ex-boss had hurt her, but she was here in Jake's arms, and he couldn't think; he could only feel. Her soft perfect lips opening for his, as he'd long dreamed. Her hands scrambling to lift the bottom of his shirt and touch his skin. He was hot, so hot, because of her, the feel of her hands on his chest almost painfully good.

He bit back a curse as he tugged her shirt over her head, then put his hands on the clasp of her strapless bra. When she nodded, he tossed it on the floor and pressed her against the door, pinning her hands above her head. Slowly, he rolled his hips against her.

She groaned and arched against him, and he was as hard as he'd ever been. Fuck, he'd been thinking about this for so long, even as he went on punishing runs in an attempt to get rid of his cravings for her. Even as he went up to his cabin and chopped wood until he couldn't move. He'd manage to rein in his desire, but just a little—and now it had been unleashed.

"Yeah, you like that?" he said.

She merely whimpered as she shut her eyes.

"Look at me, Sierra." He couldn't have her pretending he was anyone else.

He kissed her again. The length of his body against hers, her bare tits against his chest. She made erotic noises that practically had him coming in his jeans.

"Yes," she moaned.

Just as hungry and desperate for him as he was for her, which was damn impressive because he'd never been this fucking hungry before.

He dipped his head to nibble at her collarbone, then moved lower to draw one stiff peak into his mouth. She moaned again as he released her nipple and licked a circle over her areola.

"Jake," she groaned.

Oh, yeah. He could get used to that.

He grabbed her ass and lifted her up; she immediately wrapped her legs around him, her back against the door. When he rolled his hips against her again, his cock pressed between her legs. She gasped and dug her nails into his back.

"You want my cock inside you tonight?" he asked.

She nodded quickly.

"So damn eager," he murmured. "You know what I want? I want to fuck you over and over again, until you can barely walk. I want to lick you and hear you cry out my name. I want to keep you here with me all night. I want it *dirty*. Will that help you forget?"

"Well, I *had* forgotten," she said with a smirk, "until you reminded me just now."

He growled, and then his mouth consumed hers so that she'd forget again. When he set her down, he reached for the zipper on her jeans and slid his hand into her pants. Christ, she was so slick and hot. Once he was inside her, it sure as hell wasn't going to last long.

The first time, anyway.

He pushed two fingers inside. She'd left Colton's an hour ago, and she'd immediately come to Jake's, and now he had his fingers in her pussy. *Filthy.* He loved it. He'd fuck her better than Colton ever had.

He removed his hands from her body. "Take off the rest of your clothes and sit on the stairs."

She removed her shoes, followed by her jeans and panties, and sat down.

"Spread your legs," he said. "Let me see you."

She obeyed, and he knelt on the floor and put his mouth on her. One slow, sloppy kiss to her pussy lips...and he wanted to do this forever.

"Fuck, you're beautiful." He slid his fingers inside her again. Her skin glistened and...*God*. When he sucked her clit, she pushed her hips against his face and made inarticulate sounds. Her fingernails bit into his shoulders as she trembled and cried out.

At her orgasm, there was an answering wave of pleasure inside him. He kept his mouth and fingers on her through her climax but slowed his pace, then sat back on his heels to admire his handiwork. Sierra, splayed on his stairs, mussed and beautiful post-orgasm.

When he stood up, she straightened as well and reached for the buckle on his belt. His erection sprang free when she unzipped his jeans. She pulled it through the slit in his boxers and fondled him. She didn't appear anywhere near sated after a single orgasm.

Good.

He was desperate to have her writhing against him, impaled on his cock.

He hissed out a breath. "Condoms. In your purse?"

"Yes."

Thank God.

When she'd put them there, she'd probably intended for them to be used with another man, but he didn't care.

She stood up, retrieved her purse, and handed him a foil packet.

"Grab the end of the banister," he said.

She did as instructed, her ass facing him. A thing of beauty.

He rolled the condom on his shaft, then leaned forward to whisper in her ear. "I'm gonna fuck you from behind. Hard and fast." He slipped a finger inside her as he spoke. "Ready?"

When she nodded, he pressed the tip of his cock to her entrance. He waited a moment, then slid inside in a single stroke, all the way to the hilt.

She cried out and gripped the banister tightly.

"Yeah?" he said, his mouth still by her ear. "You like how I feel?"

Eagerly, she nodded again.

He thrust slowly. Sex used to be a semi-regular occurrence for him, but it had been well over a year now, and Christ, she felt amazing.

She was the only one he wanted from now on.

Unable to restrain himself any longer, he picked up the pace, and she met his strokes. Their moans and gasps mingled with the slap of his body against hers. He kept one hand on her hip; the other felt up her breasts, and with one last thrust, he was coming inside her. Pouring himself into her.

He breathed heavily as he withdrew. After turning her around, he reached out to slide a lock of sweaty hair back from her face.

He didn't ever want to let her go.

"You look well fucked," he said.

"And whose fault is that?"

He smirked.

"I hope that doesn't mean you're already done," she said.

"No." He tilted her chin up with the tip of his finger. "I'm just getting started."

[15]

I'M JUST GETTING STARTED.

Yes. That was what Sierra wanted to hear.

Earlier, he'd spoken of fucking her until she could barely walk…and it was exactly what she needed. One long night of passion.

Based on what had happened so far, Jake was more than capable of delivering.

He smacked her ass. "Head upstairs. My bedroom's on the third floor."

"Bossy, aren't you?" she said.

"You like it."

She couldn't argue with that, though she wished to be contrary, in part because he might spank her again.

"Do I?" she said saucily, putting a finger to her lips.

He slapped her ass once more. "Let's go."

She stumbled up the stairs, her legs like jelly. The old wooden stairs creaked, as they did in her house. He followed behind her, probably staring at her ass, so she wiggled her hips to put on a show.

"You want me to take you here?" he growled.

She truly believed he'd do it, and she gloried in his lust for her.

"A bed sounds nice," she said, but she continued to wiggle her hips.

When she reached the second floor, she walked down the hallway to the next staircase. He continued to follow her like a wolf stalking its prey, preparing to pounce.

She shivered in anticipation.

In his bedroom, she climbed onto the bed, lay on her back, and did something she knew would drive him wild. Something she didn't do with every man she slept with because she was too self-conscious, but that didn't bother her now.

She gave her finger one long lick, then she dipped her hand between her legs and ran that finger over her slit.

Jake stood at the end of the bed. His eyes darkened, and he thrust a hand through his short hair.

She grinned before sliding her finger inside and slowly moving it in and out.

"Enjoying the view?" she asked, adding a second finger.

He didn't reply. Instead, he shed the rest of his clothes—he hadn't taken off his pants and boxers when he'd fucked her, but they were off now, revealing his fine body. Not a carefully-sculpted body with perfect abs, but a strong, compact one.

Oh my.

She was still struggling to pull herself together when he climbed onto the bed and prowled toward her on hands and knees.

"My turn." He shoved her hand out of the way, replacing her fingers with his own, and kissed her mouth. Moisture dripped down her thighs as she bucked her hips. He plundered her mouth, his tongue sweeping inside, and then it was gone, his head moving down, down, down…

Sierra had never seen a man eat pussy the way Jake did. Like he was starving and she was the best thing he'd ever tasted. There was something so hot about seeing him between her legs, lips and tongue feasting on her.

She squirmed against him. "Jake…"

He withdrew.

"You bastard," she said, for a very different reason than she'd said it earlier that evening.

He crawled up the bed, his cock jutting toward her. He stopped when the tip was an inch from her lips. "Suck it good, and I'll let you come again."

"So bossy," she muttered, but she immediately took him in her mouth—she really was hungry for him. He'd come inside her not long ago, and he was already hard again.

He fed her more of his cock. "I want you to gag on it. That okay with you?"

Her inner muscles clenched. "Yeah."

He started fucking her mouth in earnest, filling her up, and when one stroke was particularly deep, she gagged and turned away from him. She didn't know why she enjoyed that, but she did. Oh, she did.

She was not a good girl. She was a mess.

And right now, it felt very, very good to be Sierra Wu.

When he knelt between her legs again, she was even wetter than before. He put a couple of fingers inside her, twisting them as he moved them in and out and sucked on her clit. It wasn't long before she was a goner.

After she spasmed around his fingers, he rolled on a condom and entered her from above. She welcomed the invasion: she wrapped her legs around him and urged him deeper, and he shot her a cocky smirk.

But he was right to be cocky, because it really did feel amazing. Like she was being split apart and pieced back together at the same time.

With his powerful body, he fucked her hard, and his kiss was as desperate as his cock, like he wanted to consume her in every way possible. She wished there was a big mirror on the wall so she could look to the side and watch him fuck her, so filthy and gorgeous.

She cried out in ecstasy a moment before he did.

~

After their third round of sex, Sierra was finally sated.

She was sure she'd want Jake again later, but at present, she was content to lie in bed with her head on his chest. Snuggling up to him was more comfortable than snuggling up to Colton. His body was firm, but there was a little padding.

Her gaze flicked to the corner. "You really do keep Big Freddy in your bedroom."

"I was wondering when you'd notice," he said mildly. "I suppose I should be flattered that it took an hour before you saw the giant alpaca. It's not Big Freddy, though—Freddy's downstairs. This is Big Frieda."

She lifted her head and shoved his shoulder. "You're joking. There's no way you have two giant stuffed alpacas."

His lips curved in a wicked smile. Far too wicked for a conversation about stuffed animals. "Of course I'm joking. No one but you could have convinced me to get one of those."

Heat—of a different sort from earlier—washed over her.

"How long have you had Moonbeam Messages?" he asked.

"Four years."

"Is it something you always wanted?

"Yeah." She ducked her head. "I always loved such stores."

"You seem embarrassed. No need."

"It's just… My family hates that I quit my engineering job, but honestly, I was so bad at it, and it was a miracle I hadn't been fired. I struggled in university, and I've forgotten basically everything I learned."

"My brother's an environmental engineer, but he likes it. It's his thing."

It was the first time she'd heard Jake speak of his family, but she supposed they hadn't had that many conversations.

"Your brother—was he at the bistro with you?"

Jake nodded.

"You two look alike," she said. "I mean, you're obviously more handsome—"

"Obviously."

"Someone's full of himself."

"How could I not be right now?"

She shoved his shoulder.

Most of her interactions with Jake were…intense. She didn't know how else to describe them. But now that they'd actually had sex and were relaxing in bed together, it was a little different.

He absently stroked her side, "*I'm* not disappointed you quit a job that was making you miserable. I know it can be difficult for a small business to survive, but it's been four years and you're still here, selling otter mugs and stuffed alpacas to unsuspecting customers. I'm proud of you."

She ducked her head again.

"Are you bad at taking compliments? You should get used to them." He curved his hand over her breast. "This is a lovely part of you. Perfect for nibbling and sucking." He swirled his tongue around her nipple.

She giggled and pushed his head away. "It's been, like, twenty minutes."

He rolled Sierra onto her back. His wolfish grin made her heart pump faster, but…

"Not yet," she said.

"Very well." He lay on his back next to her, arms behind his head. "I'm sure you'll be *gagging* for it soon enough."

"You're impossible, you know that?"

He shrugged from his supine position, but then he said, more seriously, "You liked that, right? You know you can stop me if I ever do something you don't want. No judgment."

He'd been careful about consent, and he'd displayed an uncanny knowledge of what dirty things would turn her on. After what had happened with Colton, that was what she'd craved. To be utterly depraved, and it had been even better than she'd imagined.

"I know." She glanced at Big Freddy again. "Why do you keep it in your room?"

"Because when I see it, I think of you, and I smile."

She shut her eyes. "You're too much."

"No, I think I'm just the right amount, and you can handle me."

He turned her onto her side and held her from behind…and she could feel him getting hard once more. She couldn't help her pride in how horny she made this man.

It wasn't long before she was ready to go again.

[16]

WHEN SIERRA WOKE up on Saturday morning, she was smiling. It was one of the Saturdays she wasn't working, thank God.

Yesterday certainly hadn't gone as expected. She was still a little pissed—only natural when your relationship of over a year went down the toilet, even if you'd been thinking of ending it anyway—but last night, surprisingly, had been one of the best nights of her life.

She'd barely let herself fantasize about sex with Jake Tong, and the real thing had been mind-blowing. Not that sex had been bad with Colton; she'd enjoyed herself. But with Jake…that was in a different league. She shivered as she remembered the hungry way he'd looked at her.

She opened her eyes, expecting to see him beside her, but there was no one else in bed. Had she imagined yesterday? Had it been a particularly vivid dream?

She was definitely in Jake's room, though, with Big Freddy in the corner.

When I see it, I think of you, and I smile.

The memory of those words made her feel all gooey inside.

But where on earth was Jake?

Since none of her clothes were in the bedroom, she peeked in his closet and pulled out the first dress shirt she found. A light blue one. She pulled it on—it landed just past her ass—and buttoned it only partially before descending the stairs.

He wasn't on the second floor.

Or the first floor.

She recalled the morning she'd woken up in Colton's bed, only to be told he was already gone on a business trip. Had Jake simply *left*?

Then she heard an odd sound coming from the basement.

Jake was releasing his frustration by using his power tools.

He'd considered a run, but he didn't want Sierra to wake up in an empty house. He assumed she'd be able to find him down here. She wouldn't be able to hear the noise from his bedroom, but when she came downstairs to fetch her clothes, she'd hear.

And then, if she wanted to leave without a word, she could.

Or if not…

Clearly, she'd chosen the latter option. She'd just stepped into the basement, not wearing her own clothes but one of his shirts.

Christ.

He turned off the circular saw before he injured himself.

Jake hadn't been unhappy to wake up with Sierra in his bed, but then the circumstances of last night had come back to him.

"Good morning," she said.

"Morning," he responded gruffly, trying not to look at the peaks of her nipples, which were pushing against the blue fabric.

She walked to the corner and peered at a small table. "This is nice. You made it?"

"Yes."

"From lawyer to carpenter?"

"It's not exactly a full-time job."

She waltzed toward him; he gripped his workbench.

"You like my outfit?" She reached out and poked his chest. "I think you do."

"Stop it," he growled.

She stepped back. "What's wrong? We had a good night together, didn't we? I was disappointed you weren't in bed this morning, to be honest."

"Last night shouldn't have happened." No matter how fucking good it had been. He'd told himself that he didn't have to hold back anymore, but he'd been wrong.

"Why not?" she asked.

"You found your boyfriend cheating. Did you even tell him it was over?"

"Of course."

"And less than an hour later, you were in my bed."

"He may have cheated on me, but I never cheated on him."

"That's not the point, Sierra."

"Please enlighten me. What's the point?" She put a hand on her hip. "That I'm a slut?"

"No, no. That's not what I'm saying." He pinched his brow. He'd truly made a mess of it. "I took advantage of you."

"What the hell are you talking about?" She threw her arms up. She hadn't buttoned all the buttons on the shirt, and he got a flash of cleavage.

He forced himself to be calm. "You'd just witnessed something upsetting—"

"Thank you for that euphemism to describe my ex getting a blowjob from two other women. Yes, it was upsetting. I wanted to forget about it. *I* threw myself at *you*. You didn't take advantage of me. I hadn't had a single drop of alcohol, in case you were wondering."

If he'd thought she'd been drinking, he wouldn't have touched her. But—

"And," she continued, "you were very clear about checking

what I wanted. This guilt you're feeling is entirely misplaced. You're treating me like I was some innocent virgin, but I'm thirty-four and I'm divorced. I've been with a number of men."

Jake filed that information away. Her age—he hadn't known how old she was. He'd guessed early thirties. And the fact that she was divorced—he hadn't known that, either.

Then he took a few deep breaths, but he didn't feel any better, even if she'd been clear she had no regrets. Because there were still other problems.

"What's wrong now?" she asked. "Do you not trust me to know my own mind?"

"No, I—"

"Or do you regret it for yourself?" She spoke more quietly now. "Every time we've seen each other, it's been clear you're attracted to me, but…"

He came around his workbench so he could stand toe to toe with her.

"The problem is that I'm in love with you," he said.

Confusion was written on her face.

Then it cleared and she laughed. "I didn't realize I had a magic vagina."

"I've been in love with you since I first laid eyes on you at that restaurant."

"That doesn't make sense."

He lifted a shoulder. "Not everything makes sense. That's why I still pursued you—sort of—even though you had a boyfriend. A boyfriend whom I just so happen to hate."

There was a longer silence.

"Oh," she said at last. "I see."

"I didn't just want a night with you. I wanted more."

"Ah. You planned to woo me with chocolates and flowers and fine wine, if I ever broke up with Colton."

"Something like that. I don't really know these things."

"My God, you're bad at this."

"I'm aware." He shoved his hands through his hair. "When you want a relationship with someone, I don't think you're supposed to begin the way I did last night."

But, fuck, the woman he yearned for had propositioned him, and it had been just as incredible as he'd imagined. His body didn't understand why he regretted it, but...

"Jake," she sighed, "I've been single for less than twenty-four hours."

"I know," he said irritably.

"I can't think about stuff like this now."

"Understandable."

"All I wanted was to wake up and fuck one more time."

"Why are you saying stuff like that?" he ground out. When she was wearing his damn shirt, like she was his girlfriend. He wanted to tear off the three buttons that were doing a poor job of covering her up and fuck her on the cold floor of his workshop. See her squirm and beg beneath him one more time. "You should go."

"Yes, I get that impression, thank you very much."

"You should also get tested, as should I. He was cheating on you and I don't know what protection you were using." Jake shut his eyes.

"Right. That's a good idea."

"Actually, don't leave yet," he said.

"Will you make up your damn mind?"

"I shouldn't let you go without feeding you breakfast."

"You shouldn't *let* me go?"

"Sorry, that came out wrong." He scrubbed a hand over his face. "Do you want coffee? How do you like your eggs?"

Sierra ought to have left, but her stomach was growling.

By the time she put on last night's clothes and entered the

kitchen, the coffee was ready. Jake handed her a mug—*the* mug, the otter one from Moonbeam Messages—before he cracked four eggs in a bowl and scrambled them with his chopsticks.

Because that was what she liked. Scrambled eggs.

She sat at the table as he cooked. It might have been cozy if it weren't for the tense silence.

This wasn't how she'd imagined the morning going. She'd thought they'd stay cocooned in his bedroom for a little while and avoid the real world. He'd get that smirk on his face before going down on her and making her scream.

Then she'd walk into the morning sunshine, feeling like she could deal with the world.

But now, his concentration was entirely on the food, not on her, and her head was spinning from what he'd said earlier.

She supposed she'd already known he had feelings for her, feelings that went beyond lust, even if they barely knew each other. But it was still hard to wrap her mind around it all.

She pulled her phone out of her purse, which had spent the night in the front hall.

Her battery was dead. Great, just great.

She could ask Jake if he had a charger, but she'd be out of here soon, and it wasn't a long trip home.

"Are you working today?" he asked.

"No," she said.

He grunted, and that was the end of their conversation. They returned to tense silence, in contrast to the argument they'd had earlier this morning and the passion of last night.

She still wanted him, and watching him cook felt like a novelty. Colton would arrange for someone else to make her breakfast; it wasn't something he did with his own two hands.

Whereas Jake did a lot of things with his own hands, based on the little she'd seen in the basement and what he'd done to her last night.

She squeezed her thighs together, still wanting.

She looked around as she sipped her coffee. It was an old house, like the one she lived in, and she'd even noted a small door for milk jug delivery. The kitchen must have been redone in the last five or ten years, though. It was simple, bright, and practical. Lots of counter space, unlike hers.

"Here." Jake slid a plate in front of her. He also put a fruit bowl with a banana and three oranges on the table. "Help yourself."

She carefully unpeeled the banana and put the tip in her mouth, pausing before taking a bite. She kept her gaze on Jake, not missing the heat in his eyes.

"Stop it," he said, "or I'll…"

"Or you'll what?"

He shook his head and looked away, and once again, they returned to silence. He efficiently shoveled food into his mouth, and she kept being distracted by him.

He seemed to have no such difficulty; he studiously avoided looking at her.

"The eggs are good," she said. "Fluffy, not overcooked."

He grunted again.

She drank her coffee. Ate her eggs.

"Are you angry at me?" she asked.

"I'm not angry at you," he said…rather angrily.

"Just at yourself?"

He didn't reply.

For some reason, she felt the need to keep this conversation going. "I'm an expert at being angry and disappointed in myself. It's not fatal, otherwise I would have expired a long time ago."

His gaze finally snapped to hers. "Don't. You've no reason to be disappointed in yourself."

"You say that like it's easy."

"I know it's not."

"But you love me, so you don't understand why I'd feel this way?"

He just stared at her.

"What?" she said. "You spoke those words. I didn't imagine it, did I?"

"No."

An unfamiliar awareness prickled her skin. She shoved her final bite of eggs into her mouth, then drained her coffee. "I should get going. Thanks for breakfast. Glad to see you're making use of your otter mug."

He followed her to the door. "Will I hear from you again?"

"Maybe. Probably." She put on her shoes. "But don't expect a text later today or tomorrow. I need some time, so I'd appreciate it if you don't contact me, even though you now have my number."

He nodded, then stepped toward her and kissed her. It was a very different kiss from the one he'd given her by the door last night.

It was a kiss of restraint.

She couldn't call it chaste, but it was probably as chaste as a kiss from Jake could feel.

She was in a bit of a daze as she walked to the subway station and waited on the platform. If people could tell she was wearing last night's clothes, she didn't care.

It wasn't a very long trip, and she was soon plodding up the steps to her house.

To her surprise, all her friends were inside.

[17]

"Oh, thank God." Rose threw her arms around Sierra.

Sierra immediately understood. Rose must have found out that Sierra hadn't spend the night at Colton's, and when she couldn't get in touch, she'd freaked out and called their friends.

"Are you okay?" Rose asked. "What happened? I was so worried."

"I'm really sorry," Sierra said. "I'm fine. I promise."

The last thing she wanted was to make Rose worry. She knew exactly what would have been going through Rose's mind, and she didn't want to bring up those memories.

She sat down on the couch, Rose and Amy on either side of her, Charlotte and Nicole on the armchairs.

"I knew you were going to Colton's," Rose said, "so I figured you might stay the night. But at ten, Colton showed up with a huge bouquet"—she gestured to the vase on the coffee table with an "I'm sorry" card—"and he was surprised you weren't here. I texted you, but you didn't reply."

"First of all," Nicole said, "what the hell did that asshole do?"

"I went to his house last night," Sierra said, "to confront him about…well, what you told me."

"What did Nicole tell you?" Amy asked.

Sierra shook her head, not wanting to get into that. "And also about various things I'd learned regarding his businesses. Instead, I found him in a limo, getting a blowjob from two other women."

The room was filled with expletives. Mostly from Charlotte and Nicole, but Rose and Amy contributed some, too, as they rubbed Sierra's back.

"They were both Asian," Sierra said. "Maybe that shouldn't matter, but it made me feel like I was just a fetish to him, and that's why he was with me. Or perhaps it was a coincidence, but I couldn't help wondering."

"I'd wonder the same thing," Nicole said.

"That fucking fucker," Charlotte muttered. Again.

Something suddenly occurred to Sierra. "Oh, no. Please say you didn't call my mother when you couldn't find me."

"Don't worry," Rose said. "She doesn't know. But where were you?"

"I'm getting to that. As soon as I stormed down Colton's driveway, I called Jake. I went to his house and we had sex. A lot of sex."

Sierra covered her face with her hands. God, she really was such a mess. She'd run into the arms of another man and hadn't bothered telling her friends where she was. And then her phone had died.

Great planning, Sierra.

She hadn't been ashamed of her actions before, but she was now.

Nicole pried Sierra's hands off her face. "Don't feel guilty for having sex. Is Jake the guy we met at the dumpling place?"

"Yes. I'd known he was interested in me, and I went to him the instant I found Colton cheating—what does that say about me? I was almost relieved by what happened because then I didn't have to feel bad about going to Jake."

"Hey," Nicole said softly. "I'm not judging you."

Sierra kept talking. "Then this morning, Jake regretted last night. He said it's not a good way to start a relationship and confessed his love for me..." She looked at Rose, remembering their previous conversation. "I'm sorry. I know you find it hard—"

Rose waved this away. "I want to hear what happened. How do *you* feel about him?"

"I don't know. I like him, but I won't be pressured into something when I'm not ready. I need time."

"That's sensible."

"Jake used to work for Colton and now hates his guts. Did I tell you that? I can't help wondering if I went to him to get back at Colton."

"By sleeping with his enemy," Nicole said. "I like it."

"To be honest," Sierra told her, "Jake's probably just a nobody to Colton now."

"So you *didn't* sleep with Jake as revenge."

"Well, maybe it was simply the idea of having sex with someone else—that part was getting back at Colton for cheating."

"Tell me this." Nicole leaned forward. "Who's bigger?"

"Nicole!" Rose said.

"Are you scandalized? Come on, you know me."

"I'm not talking about this anymore," Sierra said.

"You know what you need?" Charlotte said. "Wine. Do you want me to buy some?"

"I've got wine." Rose ran to the kitchen, then came back with a bottle of white and two glasses. She made another a trip for three more glasses.

"None for me," Amy said. "I need to work on my thesis this afternoon."

Everyone else was happy to drink. Sierra was given the first glass, and she took a healthy swallow before her friends raised their glasses.

"To Sierra," Nicole said. "May she never again have an asshole cheat on her."

"What do you want to do with the bouquet?" Charlotte asked. "It's pretty, but…"

"I'm definitely not keeping it," Sierra said. "One of you can take it, if you like."

"Uh-uh. We're going to destroy it. We'll cut it up!" Charlotte sounded disturbingly gleeful. "We can pretend we're cutting his balls. Or heart."

"I've heard that one-fifth of CEOs are psychopaths," Nicole said.

For some reason, this made Sierra guffaw.

"Cutting them up is an excellent plan," Rose said. "We can make 'fuck billionaires' potpourri." She looked excited by the idea.

Sierra's friends were doing a good job of making her feel better—in a completely different way from Jake.

Rose grabbed two pairs of scissors from the kitchen and handed one to Sierra. Sierra picked up a gerbera daisy and cut the pink flower in half. It felt wrong, but good in a way.

Nicole applauded her.

"When Colton showed up here last night," Sierra said, "what exactly did he say?"

"Just to tell you he was sorry," Rose replied.

"Do you think he believes that I should want him back because he's a billionaire? And that I should put up with shit like this because he can buy me diamonds?"

"Maybe," Nicole said, "but fuck him."

Sierra cut into a large, fragrant flower that she didn't recognize. "My mom is going to be so unhappy with me."

"I feel like a bad influence," Charlotte said, "but don't listen to your mother. Seriously. She makes you miserable."

"Doesn't change the fact that tomorrow is Mother's Day and she's going to ask about him. I don't want to lie."

"If you need someone to cheer you up after you see your mother, I'll volunteer, but perhaps someone else is better suited to the task."

"Pick me!" Amy said. "Look, I'm such a good friend that I'll destroy these flowers better than anyone else."

Sierra smiled. Her anger at Colton was fading, and though she wouldn't say she was entirely over him, it was a small pain in her heart now.

Sierra hadn't wanted to come to dim sum today. The last thing she needed was to deal with her family. However, if she skipped this one, she'd never hear the end of it.

Things had started going wrong before she'd even gotten to the restaurant: she'd waited thirty minutes for a bus that was supposed to come every ten minutes. As a result, even though she'd given herself extra time, she'd arrived late and Ma had shot her dirty looks before saying, "Ah, so nice of you to join us. I was beginning to think you didn't care about me on Mother's Day."

Po Po had merely sniffed in a way that said, *You are dead to me.*

After that, everyone had turned their attention to Lincoln and Rachel, and they'd ignored Sierra, as was preferable.

Alas, her luck could only hold out for so long.

"So, Sierra," Ma said, after Auntie Marlene had bragged about Rachel for a while, "how is Colton Sanders?"

Her tone of voice said, *You better not disappoint me.*

Sierra was used to that tone and used to disappointing her mother, so it didn't scare her. Too much.

"I caught him cheating and we broke up." She reached for the har gow. "What's new with you?"

"Sierra!" Ma screeched. "What am I going to tell everyone?"

"I don't know," Sierra said blandly. "Not my problem. You were the one who decided to tell them in the first place."

"But of course I had to tell Cece! And Ellen and—"

"Yeah, yeah, I get it, you told everyone."

"Maybe he wasn't cheating on you," Ma said. "It could be a misunderstanding. I hear men and women can be friends? It doesn't make sense to me, but—"

"He was definitely cheating."

"Did you see him *kissing* someone else?" Rachel's eldest child asked, wide-eyed.

"Uh, yeah," Sierra said. "Let's say that." She stuffed the too-hot har gow in her mouth.

Rachel raised her eyebrows and mouthed, *Sorry.*

"You can forgive him," Ma said, not to Sierra's surprise, though she'd thought Ma would wait a little longer to say it. "It's not a big deal. Men cheat all the time."

Sierra glanced at her father, who was eating and seemed oblivious to the conversation.

"Not happening," she said.

Ma leaned forward and whispered—well, what counted as a whisper for her—"You should do all the weird sex stuff that you refused to do before."

Who said I refused to do anything? But Sierra didn't say that out loud.

"Auntie!" Rachel said. "Not here. Please." She gestured to the children at the table.

Lincoln's baby shrieked in agreement and burst into tears.

Sierra wanted to sink into the floor. She should have lied and said Colton was fine, then told her mother the truth over the phone so everyone else didn't have to hear all this nonsense.

Ma clucked her tongue. "You think it's every day a man like Colton Sanders will look at you? You won't have the chance again."

"I don't need to be with a super rich man," Sierra said.

"I'm not just talking about super rich men! You're getting old. Looking your age."

"I still get carded all the time."

"All the time? Aiyah, how much alcohol do you drink?"

"Not enough," Sierra muttered.

"I'm sure Sierra can handle this on her own," Rachel said.

"I don't think so," Ma retorted. "She's not a doctor like you!"

Auntie Marlene beamed, proud of her daughter, while Sierra slumped in her chair, then set about filling her plate.

Yes, she was with family, but she felt lonely.

"Ma told me to forgive Colton," Sierra said when she came home and found Rose putting away the dishes.

"She wants you to be with a man who cheats on you?" Rose asked.

"She wants me to be with someone who has as much status as Colton, and she doesn't care if I'm happy. She never does. It's all about money and what other people will think."

"I'm sorry. My mother never would have said something like that."

Sierra remember what day it was.

Shit.

"No, *I'm* sorry," she said. "I know it's tough for you. You didn't want to go to Ottawa for Mother's Day?"

Rose shook her head. "Not this year, since I just visited in April." She picked up a bowl. "You can complain about your mom, it's fine."

Rose had grown up in Ottawa and had returned there after university, but ten years ago, Rose's mother had died by suicide, and about a year later, Rose had decided to move to Toronto. The rest of her family was still in Ottawa.

"Please don't tiptoe around me." Rose put away the last plate. "It's been a decade."

"But it doesn't go away. I know that."

"Still. I'm better at coping than I used to be."

Sierra wasn't sure what to say, so she wrapped her arms around Rose, and they held each other for a minute.

"How did everyone else react?" Rose asked. "My dad and brothers would be furious if someone cheated on me."

"I'm not sure my dad was paying attention. My brother didn't say much. Probably just glad I'm no longer dating a billionaire because it was taking attention away from him."

"Your family is wild."

"Tell me about it."

"You'll find someone better. Maybe Jake, maybe not. But you will." Rose looked away. "You know, for all the problems I had with my mom, like how she basically didn't believe in mental illness and wouldn't let me get treatment…" She swallowed audibly. "I know she would have told me that, too, and I would have believed it, coming from her. It's complicated."

Sierra rubbed her friend's shoulder. "Want to watch a movie together tonight?"

Rose nodded.

"I'm sorry I made you worry on Friday. I know it reminded you…"

"It's okay," Rose said. "But next time, let me know if you won't be home for the night."

"I will," Sierra promised.

Her family might not have her back, but she was lucky to have her friends.

[18]

Jake had never imagined this version of hell.

Both Quinton *and* Lewis trying to give him dating advice.

Quinton's visit had been planned. They'd been sitting on the porch, drinking their beers, when Lewis had walked up, saying something about stopping by for a visit because he happened to be in the neighborhood.

"So, let me get this straight." Lewis sipped his water. "She caught Colton cheating, she immediately came here, you had sex."

"Yeah, I thought I made that clear," Jake said.

"Never be the rebound guy," Quinton said. "Haven't you heard that before?"

"Sounds familiar."

"Since you're unaware of what he means," Lewis said, as though Jake hadn't spoken, "let me show you." He pulled out his phone, did a quick search, and turned it toward Jake.

9 signs you're in a rebound relationship

8 reasons you don't want to be a rebound

Jake tensed. He knew it was silly to be bothered by this, but he didn't like it when Lewis assumed he didn't know things.

Lewis clicked on the first link. "Let's see. 'Did it start soon after a breakup?' She literally went from his house to yours. 'Lots of sex.' Ooh, 'Talking about their ex all the time.' And, 'Never talking about their ex.'"

"Yeah, yeah, I get it," Jake grumbled. "Everything is on that list. If I want something more, I shouldn't have slept with her immediately after she ended a relationship, I'm aware."

"You know, relationships start in all sorts of weird and wonderful ways," Quinton said. "Melody has a friend whose now-husband bumped into her on the street and spilled orange juice all over her, which doesn't sound like a great way to begin a relationship, but—"

"Um, I think that's from a movie. Was her friend Julia Roberts?"

"Shut up. I was trying to be encouraging."

"You haven't told us how you first met Sierra," Lewis said.

"Right." Jake paused. "You know how I was talking to her at the French bistro? That was actually when I met her. Before you and Victoria arrived, I saw this beautiful woman sitting alone at a table, and I just *knew*."

"Maybe you only want to get back at Colton."

"No," Jake said, his grip on his beer can tightening. "It's not like that. And she wasn't with him when I first saw her."

"Mm-hmm."

"Why do you sound so skeptical?"

"I think you're confused about your feelings. Was I interested in Victoria the first time I laid eyes on her? Sure, but I wasn't in love with her. Besides, you haven't wanted a relationship in *years*, and this woman happens to be Colton's ex. Quite the coincidence. Perhaps a quick rebound is all it's meant to be."

Too bad Jake's beer can wasn't empty so he could crush it in his hand. He'd changed, but maybe his brother would never see it that way. "I know I want more. How do I make it happen?"

"Buy her dozens of scented candles."

"Send her a singing telegram," Quinton suggested.

"Flash mob outside her store," Lewis countered.

"Ooh, good one. Better yet, combine all those ideas, then get a basket of puppies, each with a word around their neck. 'Will you be my girlfriend, even though you dated my evil ex-boss?' Twelve words if I've counted correctly, so you'll need twelve puppies."

"Yeah, no," Jake said. "You guys are no help. I'm serious about this."

"Look," Lewis said, "this woman dated Colton Sanders for a while. I suspect she's enjoying you for now, but you're not her type for a long-term relationship. You're not—"

"Rich enough?" Jake spat. "You think that's all she cares about? You don't know her at all." He curled his hand into a fist.

"Hey, hey," Quinton said. "Easy, you guys."

"I do care for Sierra, very much." Jake gritted his teeth. "Even if it doesn't make sense to you, Lewis. I don't want to be her short-term rebound guy."

He didn't admit that his brother's words had put doubts in his head.

Did he really feel as much for Sierra as he thought he did? Was he just trying to get back at Colton?

"When was the last time you talked to her?" Quinton asked.

"Last weekend. When she left the morning after, she said she needed some space."

"Well, then. What else can you do? She'll come to you when she's ready."

Yeah, Jake knew he'd just have to wait, but it had been a week.

He looked down at his beer can and said the thing that he'd been turning over in his mind for the past several days. "What if I'm just bad at relationships?" Lewis probably thought so, but Jake was directing this at Quinton. "What if my lack of experience will make me fuck up over and over? I told her I can give her things that Colton can't. Like time. Loyalty. But…"

"Hey." Quinton slapped his back. "Will you be the perfect

boyfriend? No. Nobody's perfect. But I'm sure you can do it. Yes, many rebounds are never anything more, but some are. Like my cousin…"

"Is this from a movie again?" Jake muttered.

"No, I promise. It's real. Maybe a lot of rebounds don't work out long-term, but it's not impossible. Just don't be a jerk. Respect her boundaries. Don't get your dick sucked by other women if you're exclusive."

"I think I can manage that much."

Jake looked at his brother, half expecting Lewis to refute his words. But his brother didn't say anything—positive or negative. Just stared at his glass of water.

Jake clenched his jaw as the tension between them continued.

Yeah, he really was bad at relationships, and not only romantic ones.

It had been two weeks since Sierra had found her boyfriend cheating on her, and things had since returned to normal. Sort of.

She no longer had a billionaire boyfriend, though it wasn't like they'd spent tons of time together on weekdays anyway. It just meant she didn't occasionally go to fancy restaurants in clothes and jewelry she couldn't afford.

Which, to be honest, was a bit of a relief.

She didn't miss Colton a lot. Every now and then, sure, but more than anything, she missed feeling like *somebody* for getting his attention.

Probably the influence of her mother, who'd called a few days ago to suggest Sierra patch things up with Colton. Ma had gone on about how awful it had been to tell her friends about the breakup. How, if Cece's daughter Grace Chau had been able to bag a billionaire, surely Grace would have managed to get to the altar with him…or get pregnant…or something. Sierra had tuned out, concentrating instead on lowering her blood pressure.

She thought back to the last few months of her relationship with Colton. He'd been traveling a lot, but that was nothing out of the ordinary. He'd also taken her to his island and told her that she was special because she wasn't just using him for his money.

She snorted.

Perhaps he'd planned the trip because he was already cheating on her and felt guilty—if Colton ever felt guilty about anything.

She hadn't heard from him since. He'd arrived at her house with those flowers, which she'd decimated over wine with her friends, and then…nothing. It didn't seem like he wanted her back. She wanted him to want her back, just so she had a chance to reject him, but he was staying away.

Probably for the best.

Sierra sipped her coffee as she looked out the window. It was a Saturday, ten minutes before opening, and her mind drifted to something completely inappropriate: sex with Jake. She imagined herself splayed out on his stairs again, everything visible to his hungry stare.

Yeah, thinking about Jake seemed to bring up more feelings than thinking about Colton, and her fantasies about him were only becoming more desperate.

She imagined him coming into the store and dragging her to the back room so he could screw her against the wall. She was wearing a dress today, which would give him easy access.

But she hadn't heard from him in two weeks. He was respecting her desire for space, so if she wanted to see him again, she'd have to contact him.

Every day, she stared at his name on her phone and thought about texting him.

I miss you.

I miss your tongue.

Every time I've used my vibrator in the past two weeks, I've thought of you.

But she couldn't actually text him any of those things, could she?

Unable to help herself, she kept thinking about it for the rest of the morning. Maybe it was silly to be afraid of a few words after what they'd done together. After all the words he'd said to her…

No, she wouldn't stay away from him any longer.

At lunch, she took a ten-minute break and pulled out her phone.

I miss you, she typed, and then her finger hovered over the screen as she debated whether to add something more…

Oh, shit! She'd accidentally sent it.

Physically, I mean, she added.

She bit into her sandwich, and she hadn't even finished chewing her first bite before she got a reply.

Are you saying you want to see me again? he asked.

Yeah. Today? I'll be finished work at 6.

You're eager.

He hadn't said yes, though.

So, are you free? she asked.

If you tell me a little more about what you miss, I could be.

You're impossible.

That doesn't answer my question.

Fine. I miss your cock inside me. Her thumbs flew across the screen. *I miss your tongue. I miss tasting myself on your lips. Happy?*

Yes. For now.

Oh, thank God.

She sent Rose a text. *Probably won't be home tonight. Going to see Jake.*

$$[\ 19\ ]$$

By the time Sierra got off the subway, she was so freaking horny.

It had been the longest afternoon ever at work—her brain kept pulling up fantasies about Jake, no matter how much she told it not to—but she was finally here, less than a ten-minute walk from his place. Her heart was beating quickly in anticipation.

And because nothing ever worked out perfectly for her, it was also raining. Hard. Apparently, April showers had just brought May showers.

She didn't see any lightning or hear any thunder, and since she didn't know how long it would keep raining like this, she wouldn't bother waiting by the station. She put up her umbrella, but within seconds, it had nearly blown inside out, thanks to the strong wind.

How lovely.

She decided to make a run for it.

The rain was so heavy that she could barely see, but there was no sense turning back now—she was already soaked.

By the time she stopped in front of Jake's house, she was

huffing and puffing, and there he was, walking into the rain from the dry porch.

What the hell was he doing?

She was rooted in place. Something about his expression...it made it difficult to swallow.

He didn't speak when he reached her; he hauled her into his arms and kissed her so thoroughly that she suddenly didn't care about being cold and waterlogged.

Because he was *here*.

She'd been thinking about being with him for two weeks, and now she didn't have to imagine it anymore. She could simply touch.

It was a solid minute of kissing before a crack of thunder drowned out the beating of rain on the pavement. She jumped.

"Let's get you inside," he said.

In the front hall, she started pulling off his clothes, and he pulled off hers. Her dress stuck to her body, but he eventually managed to drag it off, quickly followed by her bra and panties.

He stood there shirtless, his chest wet and glistening in the low light.

"So you missed me," he murmured, tugging her close. "My cock, my tongue...that's what you said, isn't it? What about my fingers?" He slipped his hand between her legs and ran a callused finger along her seam.

When she nodded, he slid that finger inside, his face just far enough from hers so she could see his wicked grin.

"I missed you, too," he said. "Every day, I wished I could be inside you again. Now that you're here, I'm going to have my fill."

She was trembling and she hardly knew why. Because she was cold? Excited? Both?

"But first, I'll warm you up." He hoisted her into his arms and walked up the stairs. All the way up to the third floor...she was impressed.

He set her down in the washroom, grabbed a fluffy towel, and began drying her off. Then he set the towel on the counter and lifted her up to sit on it.

When he dropped his pants and boxers and started stroking himself, her mouth went dry. God, it was so fucking sexy to watch him touch himself. In fact, she found everything he did sexy. Never had a man just oozed sex in front of her like this.

"I jerked off in the shower so many times," he said, "as I thought about devouring you and fucking you in every way possible."

She moaned, and he got on his knees and gave her pussy one long lick. She put her hands behind her on the counter and kept her gaze on him. Pressure built inside her, threatening to explode. Her breath was coming quickly, and then he slid a finger inside her and twisted it…and his tongue worked furiously on her clit.

"Jake!" she screamed as her body shook, as she tingled all over from the soles of her feet to her fingertips.

He stood up, and she expected a cocky smirk on his face, but instead, it was just hunger. His lips were wet, not from the rain but her moisture. He kissed her mouth, his tongue sweeping inside to meet hers, and she clutched him with one arm. There was only him…and her…nothing else mattered.

Then he was back on his knees, feasting on her again, like he needed this more than anything else in the world. She closed her eyes and just let herself feel. The waves of pleasure…up and down, up and down…but slowly building…

She screamed again as her second orgasm crashed over her.

He put on a condom and slid inside while the aftershocks were still rolling through her.

This was too much.

But it was also perfect.

He fucked her with long, deep strokes, one hand gripping the counter, the other on her back. The way this man moved… God, it should be illegal.

She kept her eyes open because of the way he was looking at her. As though she was all that fucking mattered, and as though he could see right into her.

See into *her*. Sierra Wu, Not a Demon Slayer.

She hadn't thought she could come again, but a moment later, she combusted. Lost track of what her body was doing and what was coming out of her mouth.

But she did register that he was growling and coming inside her at the same time, and that caused joy to explode within her.

"You look like one of those weird jellied salads from back in the day," Jake said.

"Shut up."

Sierra was lying prone on his bed, her face turned in his direction, though her eyes were closed. She'd been like this for at least twenty minutes, ever since he'd carried her here from the washroom.

She marveled that his body could function after fucking her on the bathroom counter like that. Hers certainly wasn't what she'd call "functional."

But it was okay. After being a little on edge for the past two weeks, she now felt blissed out.

He put his arm around her, and they stayed there in silence for a while.

"You hungry?" he asked at last. "There's Chinese food on Gerrard, plus a Vietnamese place that I order from sometimes. Greek food on the Danforth, of course."

"Vietnamese sounds good. Pick something for me. I don't think I have the brainpower to make more decisions."

"I usually get the vermicelli with spring rolls and grilled pork."

"Sounds good."

She felt him get out of bed, presumably to find his phone, and she didn't even bother looking up to watch him walk naked across the room—she was too jelly-like.

Some indeterminate time later, he climbed back into bed. "It'll be here in half an hour."

"Mmm." She finally opened her eyes. "I suppose we should talk."

～

Yes. Talking. They should do that.

But as soon as Jake had seen Sierra in the rain, he'd wanted to touch her everywhere and make her come...which he'd now done.

"As you know," she said, "I just got out of a relationship. I'm not looking for anything serious. Just casual."

His heart dropped, even though this was expected. "By casual, you mean sex and takeout?"

"And I'd like to stay overnight again, if you promise not to freak out."

"I promise."

Last time, she'd found him in the basement, and he'd confessed his love. Though he didn't admit it, that confession embarrassed him now.

He'd been replaying his conversation with Lewis, and he'd eventually concluded that he didn't *really* love Sierra. He merely liked her and was attracted to her—and intrigued by her.

Love. That seemed to be taking things a bit far. Could he be sure he wanted a serious relationship at this point?

No, casual would be good for now.

"Works for me," he said, ignoring the lump in his chest.

It was still raining outside, though it didn't sound like it was coming down nearly as hard anymore. But inside, he was cocooned under the blankets with Sierra.

"I don't expect exclusivity," she said. "Just so you know."

"Okay." Though he had no intention of sleeping with anyone else. Couldn't imagine doing so. Even if he wasn't exactly sure how he felt, he knew that much.

"Seeing you once a week, Saturday or Sunday night, would work for me."

He nodded.

"You're positive you're okay with that?" She didn't mention his confession, for which he was thankful.

"Yeah. One night a week of having you all to myself? Sounds pretty damn good to me." He'd happily take more, of course, but that seemed greedy.

She rolled onto her back. "Next Sunday. You available then?"

"We're making plans more than a week in advance now?"

"It'll be nice to see you after dim sum with my family." She sighed. "I'm an endless disappointment to them, and the one thing I had going for me was a rich boyfriend. They're upset that they gave me all those opportunities only to have me open a little store. Well, I say 'they' but it's my mainly my mom. Worse, I'm divorced and have no kids."

"How long were you married?"

"Three years." Jake was prepared to hear about another guy he'd want to beat up, but then she said, "We're better off as friends. He's a decent person, just not for me. He's married to someone else now, and I'm happy for him."

Jake relaxed his fist. He couldn't help the jealousy that sprang up inside him, but he didn't want to punch the guy in the face.

"My brother," Sierra said, "is perfect in my family's eyes. Engineer. Wife and kids. I struggle for any scrap of pride in my mother's voice when she talks of me. Instead, I have to hear about Lincoln, and my cousin Rachel—who's a doctor—and my mom's friend's daughter. I never measure up to any of them, though when I was dating a billionaire, I came close." She shook her head. "You don't need to listen to me whine."

"Hey," he said, putting his hand on her cheek. "I just want you to know…I can't imagine being disappointed in you."

"Oh, just you wait."

"No, I mean it. I think you're amazing."

"Because you want to fuck me again, and you know I'm easy when it comes to you."

The corner of his mouth tipped up. "I do enjoy when you throw yourself at me, but that's not why I'm saying it." He brushed his thumb over her cheek and captured her gaze, needing her to understand. "I like your store, and it's *yours*, no one else's. You did it despite what they wanted. I know that takes strength."

"I did it after failing at everything else."

"No, after you discovered it wasn't right for you."

"I always knew it wasn't right for me. I just wanted them to be proud of me for once, rather than thinking I was frivolous." She shook her head again then burrowed against him.

He ran his hand up and down her back. "Are you close with anyone in your family?"

"I get along best with my grandfather. He's ninety-four and losing his memory though, and it's tough. My cousin brought him to my store once, but no one else has come." Rachel had also visited by herself a second time—she'd bought a few things and hadn't even asked for a family discount.

"But they all live in the Toronto area?"

"Yeah. I told my mom I wanted her to see it, although I dreaded it at the same time because I knew she'd pick apart everything. She didn't even try to stop by, not until the week I was away with Colton."

"Yet you told me never to visit again."

"I was dating another man," she said.

"But you were tempted by me?"

"Please don't make me say it."

"I won't. I'll just make you suck my cock later."

She released an unsteady breath.

"You like when I boss you around, don't you?" he said.

"Maybe a little."

He slipped his hand between her legs. "Seems you like it more than that."

God, he could never have enough of how wet she got for him.

Even though it took a lot of effort, he removed his hand. "Not now. Our food will be here soon, and we'd better get dressed. I suppose you'll have to wear something of mine since your clothes are drenched in a pile by the door."

He walked over to the dresser and didn't miss the way her gaze followed him, the way she licked her lips.

It was going to be difficult to make it through dinner.

He pulled out a T-shirt, boxers, and shorts for himself, then went to the closet and removed the dress shirt that she'd worn two weeks ago.

"This," he said, "is the only thing you're allowed to wear for the rest of the day."

"What if I'm extra naughty and put on a pair of your pants?"

"Then I might have to spank you."

He watched her face carefully and noted a flare of heat.

She was going to be so sore tomorrow, and he had a feeling she'd enjoy that very much.

When Jake awoke at eight the next morning, Sierra was lying in bed next to him. It was a sunny day, and the morning sunlight filtered through the blinds and illuminated her face.

His chest ached at how pretty she was.

Unlike two weeks ago, he didn't go to the basement and turn on some power tools. No, he just stayed in bed. Without regrets.

He wasn't entirely sure where this would lead, but they'd

talked, and he was content to be in the moment with her. Right now, it was easy to push aside thoughts of the future.

Instead, he thought of all the ways he could make her feel good today. Sexually, of course, but he also intended to cook her breakfast, and this time, their morning meal wouldn't be filled with uncomfortable tension.

She needed to know just how amazing she was in every way. Her family had made her believe otherwise, and he wanted to have *words* with them. While his family certainly wasn't perfect, hers seemed to be on a whole other level.

Her eyes fluttered open.

"Hey," he said softly, almost afraid he'd spook her if he spoke any louder.

"Hey." She ran a hand through her mussed hair. "You're still in bed."

"I am."

There was a beat of silence.

He'd woken up with many women in his bed before, sometimes more than one at a time. That was back in the days when he'd been working for Colton, when seducing women was a status symbol of sorts. Jake had enjoyed the sex, but he'd done it partly just to show that he could.

Although waking up with someone in his bed wasn't an unfamiliar situation, it was different—more intimate—with Sierra. And not just because he hadn't had sex in quite a while before her.

It was slower and gentler than last night, and then they got dressed—he'd dried the clothes she'd been wearing yesterday—and he made her breakfast.

By the time she left, it was almost noon, and after she kissed him on the cheek, she said, "You're no longer banned from Moonbeam Messages."

"I can visit you and bug you whenever I like?"

She gave him a stern look. "That's not what I said. But if you do happen to walk in, I won't kick you out, and I won't make you buy over a hundred dollars' worth of stuff."

"Good. Big Freddy might get jealous if I bring home another giant stuffed animal."

She laughed as she walked down the stairs from the porch, a spring in her step.

And this time, he wouldn't have to wait two weeks to see her again.

[20]

THE FOLLOWING SATURDAY, Sierra was about to leave for work when she found something on the porch that dampened her mood: a heart-shaped box of chocolates. It was accompanied by an "I'm sorry" card with Colton's signature. He hadn't written anything personal, just signed his name.

She unblocked his number so she could send him a quick text: *I'm not interested, you bastard.*

When he still hadn't replied by the time she closed for the day, she blocked his number again, then headed to meet Rose, Charlotte, Nicole, and Amy at Ossington Cider Bar.

"Can I get you started with some drinks?" the server asked the table.

Sierra was about to pipe up with her order for the whiskey barrel-aged cider, but before she could speak, Amy said, "Just give us two minutes." After the server left, Amy leaned forward. "I have something to tell you all."

Any thoughts of Colton's half-hearted gesture flew out of Sierra's brain. She had a feeling she knew what her friend's news was.

Amy's pregnant.

When Amy had declined wine at the fuck-Colton-Sanders event four weeks prior, it had occurred to Sierra, but she hadn't thought much of it.

But now…

"I'm pregnant!" Amy said.

"Oh my God!" Nicole immediately got up to give her a hug. "Congratulations."

"Congrats!" Sierra was next to hug Amy, followed by Charlotte and Rose.

"I'm about nine weeks," Amy said, "so it's still early. Please don't tell anyone else. But it's hard to stay quiet when I keep puking, and when I have to watch what I'm eating and drinking. I hope I can defend my thesis without being sick in the middle. We weren't going to start trying until next year, once I'd been at my new job for a little while, but…" She giggled. "I'm happy."

"And Victor?" Sierra asked.

"Oh, he's over the moon. Less outwardly excited than I am, of course, but he's thrilled. I think we'll try to have two, but I should probably see how I deal with this one first."

The night ended a little earlier than usual, as Amy was tired. She, Rose, and Sierra took an Uber home, and Sierra gave her friend one last hug before Amy skipped up the steps to the house she shared with her husband.

Next door, Sierra and Rose tugged off their shoes.

"Let's get drunk." Rose shuffled into the living room and slumped on the couch. "We're already halfway there, so it shouldn't take long."

Sierra frowned. "Are you okay?"

"No," Rose said miserably. "I should be, but I'm not. The peach soju in the kitchen—could you get it?"

It was rare for Rose to want to get drunk. Sierra grabbed the soju and poured them each a small glass before sitting down next to Rose.

"Do you think Amy could tell?" Rose asked. "That I was on the verge of tears?"

"I couldn't tell, and I've known you for much longer than she has."

"That's good." Rose tossed back some soju. "I'm happy for her, I truly am—"

"I know."

"But Amy inherited a house in Toronto, met a guy, got married, got pregnant…all in, like, two years. She's younger than us! And I…" Rose shook her head. "I can't get pregnant."

"Oh, Rose."

"It's not what you're thinking. I have no reason to believe I physically can't get pregnant, but in the past year, I've realized it's probably the last thing I should do. For my mental health. I'm not sure I could manage all the physical changes, but more than that, it's the thought of caring for a baby. Even though I love babies, the idea of looking after a newborn who wakes up and needs to be fed every two hours…that's basically my version of hell. It's easy to imagine I wouldn't sleep at all, and when I don't sleep, my mental health plummets, and what if I get postpartum depression? All of that terrifies me. And I don't have a mom to help me, and…"

Rose started crying, and Sierra's heart ached. She put an arm around her friend.

"I don't know if I want children," Rose said, "I just *know* I cannot give birth and look after babies—and not having that option upsets me."

Yeah, Sierra could understand that, even if it was very different from her own situation.

"Not that I think people with mental illness should never have kids," Rose continued, "but for me, getting pregnant isn't a good idea. Maybe I could adopt slightly older kids one day, but I worry about fucking them up, too. So many people give their kids lots of trauma, and…I don't know. I think I could be a good mother most of time? Maybe? But the rest of it…"

"Nobody's the perfect parent. It's impossible."

"I know, I know, but like…is that why you don't want kids? Or you just never particularly had the desire?"

"Never had the desire. But, not gonna lie, I think my parents messed me up a *lot*."

Rose giggled. She was definitely on her way to drunk. The peach soju was dangerous stuff. It went down almost like juice, but it was over 10% alcohol.

"For the record," Sierra said, "you're a much more self-aware and thoughtful person than my mother. I know you could do a better job at it than her."

"Even with older kids, it might lead to me having a breakdown." Rose shook her head. "Besides, I don't want to be a single parent, not in my situation. I need a man." She laughed. "But I haven't had a relationship in over a decade."

Sierra opened her mouth, but Rose held up a hand.

"No platitudes, remember? They feel like lies, but if I say I'm not hopeful, people claim it's just my depression talking." Rose gulped more of her booze, then looked surprised that her glass was empty. She poured herself more, her coordination worse than usual, before taking off her glasses and rubbing her eyes. "God, I'm a mess tonight."

"That's okay." Sierra held up her glass. "We can be messes together."

"I'm glad it's you," Rose said, sagging against her. "Charlotte wants kids, and Nicole said she'd like to have a kid—just one, though—with David. But you don't."

"And I'm not in a relationship, either."

"No, it's just sex, right?"

"Yeah." Sierra had seen Jake twice more since she'd gone to his house in the rain.

"I hope it's really good sex." Rose giggled again. "Is he better than Colton?"

"Yeah, but that might be chemistry, not skill level. Though he's particularly talented with his tongue."

Sierra covered her mouth after speaking. She didn't usually share such things with her friends, but it was just the two of them, and wow, this soju was potent.

"You mean when he goes down on you," Rose said, "not just kissing?"

"Yep."

"Does he do it every time?"

"He does do it a lot."

Oh, God. Now Sierra was both horny and drunk. It was hard to think of Jake going down on her without getting turned on.

"I've never had oral sex," Rose said. "I mean, I've never received it. But I hear it's excellent."

"You never… *What?* That's a travesty. Assuming it's something you want, of course."

"It is. Does he…" Rose gestured vaguely with her hands. "Does he enjoy it? Or does he just enjoy you returning the favor?"

"It's like he wants to *devour* me. Whenever we see each other, we basically jump each other right away. Like, we can barely talk until we've done it." Sierra clapped a hand over her mouth again.

"I have no idea what that's like. For someone to be that desperate to touch me."

"It's never been this way before—not to this extent at least. Not with Colton, not with Justin. I'm sure it won't last. I don't see how it could."

"Even if it can't last, I wish it would happen to me." Rose looked wistfully toward the window.

"I want to say that one day, it will, but I have a feeling you wouldn't like that."

"Correct. Not hoping…it helps me cope, actually. Being disappointed over and over again is too much to bear, and besides, it's not like I really need a guy who's all over me. My desires are modest."

"But don't *settle*, Rose," Sierra said. "I did that, and now I'm divorced."

Rose nodded and had more of her soju. Then she gave Sierra a hug—well, more like she half fell on top of Sierra. "Are you sure Amy didn't notice I was sad?"

"I'm pretty sure."

"I'm good at pretending sometimes."

Sierra stroked Rose's hair. "I know."

"Are you seeing Jake tomorrow?"

"Yeah."

"Good. Get all the dick you can."

"Rose!" Sierra started laughing because that was something Rose would never, ever say if she was sober.

"Dammit." Rose lifted up the bottle. "We finished the soju. Maybe I'll grab the vodka."

"Uh-uh. I think we're good for tonight. You gonna be okay?"

"Yeah. Think so," Rose slurred. "But I'm hungry. Do we have those egg roll cookies?"

Wednesday morning, as Sierra organized the washi tape before opening the store, she found herself wishing she could see Jake after work.

No. It was best not to get too involved with someone yet. It had only been a month since her breakup. They had plans to see each other on the weekend—there was no need to see him earlier.

Just before six o'clock, the chimes above the doors tinkled, and Sierra groaned. It was a pain when someone came in right before closing. For whatever reason, it was always a person who wanted to amble through the small store and pick up every single card, and she wasn't in the mood for that today.

She forced a smile as she turned toward the door, and suddenly, that smile wasn't so forced.

"Jake!"

She was so freaking happy to see him...because of all the orgasms she anticipated. That was the reason, right?

Jake wore a polo shirt and jeans. He didn't prowl toward her the way he sometimes did; instead, he looked around uncertainly, and her heart squeezed.

"Is it okay that I'm here?" he asked.

"Yes! It's fine. I told you that, didn't I? Convenient that you came right before I started closing up."

"Mm-hmm. Very convenient." Now he was looking at her like he had X-ray vision and could see under her clothes.

Her skin prickled, and her nipples tightened.

She flipped the sign on the door. "There are rules. Nothing is happening at my place of work—"

"But you're the boss." He approached her and stroked a finger down her cheek.

"I said—"

"What? This is G-rated."

"What's going on in your mind right now isn't G-rated."

"Well, no."

Last time he'd been in Moonbeam Messages, she'd tried not to admit to herself how much she wanted to touch him, but now, things were different.

"Twenty minutes," she said firmly. "I need twenty minutes to finish up here. Then we can go to my place."

"I thought I was the bossy one?" He trapped her against the counter, and oh God, why did she want this man so much?

"Jake!"

"Fine, fine. How about I wait outside?"

Twenty minutes later, as promised, she locked up the store

and they headed north. It felt strange to be walking in public with him. Not in a bad way, just…strange.

To be honest, it was nice being out with someone who wouldn't be randomly recognized on the street. Unlike, say, just pulling a name out of thin air here, Colton Sanders.

When they arrived at her house, they couldn't tear each other's clothes off in the front hall, since Sierra had a roommate.

"Rose?" Sierra said after she stepped inside.

Rose was in the kitchen, posing Fred next to the egg roll cookie tin.

"Hey," Rose said. "I—Oh. Hi, Jake!"

Jake held out a hand. "Rose, right? I think we met over dumplings."

"Yes! I'm Rose. This is my alpaca, Fred. He's making content for his Instagram account. I hear you have an alpaca, too?" Rose was talking faster than usual.

Sierra took Jake's hand. "I'll be upstairs if you need me, Rose."

She led Jake to her bedroom on the third floor and closed the door. She'd expected him to ravish her right away, but instead, he took a seat on her bed.

"Did I do something wrong?" he asked. "She seemed nervous."

Oh.

To be honest, Sierra was touched at how he appeared a little vulnerable. It seemed important to Jake that her friends liked him.

Colton had never worried about her friends. Didn't even show up half the time he was supposed to meet up with them.

She sat beside Jake. "The other day, Rose and I got drunk." They'd both been in rough shape the next morning, and Rose had sworn she'd never drink peach soju again. "We were sharing a few things we wouldn't normally share, and I may have mentioned how you really like going down on me. I think that's why she couldn't look you in the eye. I'm sorry."

He chuckled. "Just wanted to make sure I hadn't screwed up."

"How would you have screwed up?"

"I don't know." He looked distant for a moment, but then he turned toward her with a wolfish grin. "You're right. I do really like going down on you."

He peeled off her clothes and showed her just how true that was.

~

Sierra lay in her bed, cuddled against Jake's side.

"Do you want kids?" she asked suddenly.

"Where did this come from?"

"Some things have happened recently… I was curious, but it's no big deal."

"I've never had an urge to, no."

It shouldn't matter—this was just a casual thing, after all—but she couldn't help being glad that he agreed with her there.

"I don't want kids," she said. "I've known that for a long time. That's partly why I married Justin. He was the first guy I'd ever dated who also didn't want kids, and it was a relief to finally date someone who was on the same page as me there. It felt like a sign, and I couldn't imagine I'd ever get more than a half-decent guy who also didn't want children."

Jake played with her hair. "It sounds like you settled."

"I did. There was no lasting passion between us, and we weren't compatible in other ways. But I won't settle again."

However, she couldn't help wondering if she'd "settled" with Colton. It seemed weird to say that about a man who was considered such a catch, but he hadn't been fully invested in her.

Huh.

"You okay?" Jake asked.

"Yeah. Just thinking."

She didn't want to bring up Colton, but it was inevitable that she'd compare them; she'd just broken up with Colton a month ago and Jake was her rebound.

She'd stayed with Colton for so long in part because of her family. Especially her mother, who didn't seem to care how Sierra was treated by men. That was pretty fucked up.

Tears streaked down her face.

"Hey." Jake raised himself above her and wiped her cheeks with his fingers.

"I don't want to talk about it," she said, trying not to sound snappy.

He didn't push. "That's okay. We won't."

It looked like it was a struggle for him to say that, like he hated the thought of anyone hurting her and would relish the opportunity to hit them over the head with a power tool. She was confident in his loyalty to her, and that made the tears flow even more.

"Sierra," he murmured as he lay down on his back and pulled her close. "I've got you."

She was crying because she felt safe to cry, whereas when she was alone, sometimes crying just felt terrifying.

But she wasn't terrified now, wrapped up in his arms. It seemed okay to be a bit of a mess, and she wasn't used to feeling that way. She was used to feeling like she was never enough.

A while later, he said, "Sorry, I have to go to the washroom. Where is it?"

She directed him down the hall, then picked up her phone. She had a text from Rachel, which was surprising as Rachel almost never texted her.

Is this your mother? The question was followed by a link to Twitter.

Sierra clicked on it. Someone had replied to one of Colton's tweets with a totally unrelated comment.

@WuMama888: *YOU CHEATED ON MY DAUGHTER. YOU ASSHOLE!*

Sierra read that over again and again. It didn't make any sense.

Her mother was on Twitter?

Her mother was actually upset that Colton had cheated on Sierra, rather than just being upset that she wouldn't forgive him?

Of course, no one was taking this tweet seriously and Colton hadn't replied. Not only did @WuMama888 not have a blue checkmark, unlike Colton Sanders, but the Twitter account had zero followers and few tweets, as though Ma had created an account for this specific purpose.

There was a warm, fuzzy feeling in Sierra's chest. She wasn't used to her mother inspiring such feelings.

She typed a response to Rachel. *Maybe???*

When Jake returned to the bedroom, she immediately showed him the tweet. "I think my mother might be trolling Colton."

Jake climbed back into bed, and she snuggled up against him. She felt strangely content, though she couldn't help worrying what dim sum would be like on Sunday.

[21]

By the time she arrived at the restaurant, Sierra was nauseous.

This, of course, was her own damn fault for looking at her phone on the bus. She should know by now, given her vast experience with TTC buses, that they were absolutely the worst vehicle for reading.

She slowly walked across the large parking lot to the restaurant. It might not be the prettiest place, but the fresh air was helping her feel better, though she was still a bit nauseous at the thought of facing her family.

They were waiting for a table when she arrived. Lincoln wasn't here yet, and foolishly, she was proud of herself for arriving before her brother.

"Sierra, why are you looking at me funny?" Ma demanded, talking loudly so she could be heard over the background noise in the restaurant. "Is something wrong with my face?

Sierra hadn't planned to bring it up yet, but she couldn't hold back. Plus, Auntie Marlene was talking to Po Po and Gung Gung, so only her mother would hear.

"Ma, are you on social media?" Sierra asked, deciding to ease into this.

"Yes, I have the Facebook. Aren't we friends?"

Right. That was part of the reason Sierra rarely used Facebook aside from updating the page for Moonbeam Messages. "What about Twitter?"

Ma looked momentarily alarmed but quickly said, "Ah, why would I do that?"

"I don't know. You tell me."

"Why are you talking such nonsense? On Twitter, you can only use two hundred and eighty characters. Not enough to say anything."

Sierra pulled out her phone. "Who's WuMama888?"

"Wah, how should I know this random person on the internet?"

Sierra read the tweet out loud. "'You cheated on my daughter. You asshole!' I dated Colton, and he cheated on me. Seems reasonable to think that tweet came from you."

"You have such silly ideas!" Ma said. "That's not me."

"Well, you've been known to lie before."

"Are you still holding the time I said there was no Pocky against me? You were nine."

"Actually, I'd forgotten about that incident, but it's not like you've been completely truthful since then."

"What a terrible thing to say to your mother."

"But you do play fast and loose with the truth," Sierra said. "On a regular basis. Why can't you admit you were on Twitter defending me?"

"I wasn't defending you," Ma huffed.

"So, you admit you wrote this tweet?"

"Aiyah, you're speaking all twisty. I didn't write that, and we won't talk about it anymore. Have you found a new boyfriend yet?"

Sierra hesitated. "No."

"Why did you have to think about it?"

"I was caught off guard by the change in topic!"

"Ah, you are such a pain."

Sierra would have pushed harder, but Lincoln and his family arrived, and their table was ready a minute later. Besides, it didn't seem like she was getting anywhere with her mother.

At one point, however, Rachel shot Sierra a knowing look, and Sierra almost burst into laughter and spilled her tea.

Po Po glared at her.

"What's so funny?" Ma demanded.

"Oh, nothing. Nothing at all." Sierra knew she didn't sound convincing, but whatever. She was positive her mother had written that tweet, even if Ma had refused to admit to it and continued to be her usual aggravating self.

"I saw Cece yesterday," Ma said. "Grace and her husband are moving to a bigger house, only five minutes from Cece."

Sierra nodded and hoped this would be over soon.

"When are you buying a house, Sierra?"

"Probably never. Prices are too high."

"Then you can move to an apartment near us."

Yeah, no. That sounded like a nightmare.

"My job is downtown," Sierra said.

"Aren't you tired of that?" Ma asked. "Time to move back to the suburbs and get a proper job. There's an engineering firm just around the corner."

"We've been through this before. It's not even the same kind of engineering that I used to do, and I'm never working as an engineer again."

By the time Sierra got on the bus to head home, she was in an even worse mood, but at the thought of visiting Jake tonight—after he had dinner with his family—she smiled. Her life seemed to revolve around seeing him. That was what she looked forward to more than anything.

She'd claimed she was keeping it casual, but was she lying to herself?

~

"Jake has a girlfriend," Lewis said.

Jake restrained himself from throwing his chopsticks at his brother's head.

They were at their parents' house, along with Victoria and Charlene, for dinner. And apparently also so Lewis could talk about Jake's personal life, like they were little kids tattling on each other again.

Jake wouldn't mind Lewis making comments about Jake's personal life if their parents were the sort to nod and say, "That's nice, dear," before moving on.

But that did not describe Mom and Dad.

"She's not my girlfriend." Jake wished he could refer to her as such—away from his parents, that was—but he suspected Sierra would feel differently, and even though she wasn't here, he felt the need to be clear on the matter. "But we're seeing each other, yes."

"If you're dating, doesn't that mean you're in a relationship?" Dad frowned.

"No. And we're not exactly dating."

"I thought 'seeing each other' and 'dating' were the same thing."

"How many times have you seen her since she broke up with Colton?" Lewis asked.

Jake shot his brother a stormy look.

Why had he even bothered trying to patch things up with his brother, when Lewis was going to do shit like this in front of their family?

"I don't understand," Mom said. "You're dating Colton's ex? You told me not long ago that he had a girlfriend."

"Jake thinks he's in love with her," Lewis supplied, "but I doubt he knows what love is."

Victoria laid a hand on her husband's shoulder and whispered in his ear.

Jake, on the other hand, started to stand, but when Charlene grabbed his arm, he sat back down. After all, Lewis had a point. What did Jake know?

He just didn't want this shit discussed in front of his parents.

"Did she cheat on Colton with you?" Mom asked.

"No," Jake said. "He's the one who cheated on her."

Mom muttered something in Cantonese. Possibly swear words, but it was hard to tell from the other side of the table. "You should invite her to meet us. I don't think I've ever heard of you having a girlfriend before—you don't tell me these things."

"I didn't tell you this time, either. Lewis did. And I don't think she's ready to meet my family. It's not like that."

"It's just sex, that's what he's saying," Lewis added.

"What the hell is wrong with you?" Jake exploded.

"Aiyah, why can't you two get along?" Mom shook her head.

"I don't know," Jake said, leaning menacingly toward his brother. "Why can't you let things go? Why did I ever tell you *anything* and believe you could treat me with respect? You just continue to be obnoxious."

"I really like the bedside tables," Charlene said to Jake. "They're perfect." Apparently, she was trying to play peacemaker.

It was very obvious to everyone what she was doing, but they went along with it.

When Jake drove home that night, he was in a bad mood. Lewis's words had gotten to him.

What on earth was Jake doing with Sierra? What was she doing with him? She'd said she wanted to keep things casual—not much more than sex, right? But she knew he wanted more, yet they never talked about it now.

At home, he read more listicles on how being the rebound was bad. *Ooh, look, this one has fourteen items rather than just six. It'll make me feel even worse. Perfect.*

And once he got on that self-loathing train, it was hard to get off.

As soon as Sierra arrived, he crushed his mouth against hers and slid his hand under her dress. He was using her to forget that he was a piece of shit. He might be a terrible person, but at least he could make her come.

But before he had the chance to do that, she dropped to her knees in the front hall, opened his pants, and took him in her mouth. He tipped his head back and groaned.

I don't deserve this. I don't deserve this.

Yet here he was, with his cock between her pretty lips.

He pulled away and rolled on a condom. Then he lifted her up, pushed aside her panties, and lowered her onto his cock. She cried out as he sank into her.

He fucked her hard against the wall. "You feel that? You like it?"

She nodded quickly.

"I know you do." He licked his finger and touched her clit while he supported her with his other hand.

When he thrust deeper, her pussy clenched around him, and he was a goner.

But once he was aware of his surroundings—and not just how good she felt in his arms—he slid to the floor and felt like shit once again.

[22]

"I'm sorry," Jake said.

Sierra frowned. "Why are you sorry?"

They'd had hot sex right inside the entrance to his house—no need to apologize for that—and now they were curled up on the couch in the living room, their clothing righted. Mostly.

"It was rough," he said, "and—"

"But you know I like it that way."

"Today was different." He shut his eyes.

Yeah, she'd sensed there was uncontrolled rage just below the surface, but she'd been happy to be his release.

"Tell me," she said softly.

He stroked her back. It was another minute before he spoke. "My brother referred to you as my girlfriend in front of our parents, even though you're not my girlfriend and he knew I wouldn't want to talk about it with our parents because they ask a lot of questions."

Sierra was all too familiar with not wanting her parents to know things.

"My brother and I were never best friends," Jake said, "but in high school and university, we got along for the most part. Then I started working for Colton, and he lost all respect for me. I don't think there's anything I can do to gain it back, even though it's been two years."

"I tried to look the other way when it came to Colton's business. I knew he was a real estate mogul who was involved in lots of other things, but I didn't try to understand. Didn't keep track of everything he did. I know that makes me sound like a bimbo, but…"

Jake shook his head. "I don't see you that way. You were focused on other matters—"

"Yeah, like how my mom would finally be proud of me. I probably seemed like a gold digger to most people."

"No. You're amazing." He spoke with a startling amount of conviction.

"You say that even though I dated your enemy."

"Well, perhaps your taste in men isn't perfect. After all, you're here with me now."

She wasn't used to him being this self-deprecating. "You need to forgive yourself, and then maybe we can figure out how to take him down together."

"I'm not sure Colton Sanders can be taken down. He gets lots of bad press, and the vast majority of it is true, but he still doesn't suffer consequences. Many people—and I admit I used to be one of them—think he must be brilliant to get to where he is. They want to be like him. A god in our capitalistic society."

"I was reading about the meat processing plant…"

"Yeah. It's bad. To be fair, I believe there are lots of problems in that industry and it's not just him, though I think he's worse than average. And some of that stuff you read in the media?" Jake smirked. "It may have been me who leaked it. But like I said, he just doesn't suffer consequences, nothing more than a slap on the wrist."

"The other day—to torture myself, I guess—I looked at

pictures from the gala and read comments people made about me and Colton."

"Those were disgusting. Now I feel like I need to wrap you in a blanket, feed you ice cream, and compliment you for twenty-four hours."

She hoped he couldn't tell that her heart was trying to leap out of her chest toward him.

Colton never would have said something like that to her. He would've just bought her a diamond necklace.

"What do you do now?" she asked, realizing she didn't know much about Jake when it came to certain things. "Other than the work you do in your basement?"

"Not much of anything. In the years I worked for Colton, I made a decent amount of money. I live in this house I bought with my ill-gotten gains, and I have savings. I did donate a bunch of my money, though, and I volunteer at the food bank every week. That's about it. I told myself I could take two years to figure out what I wanted to do next. It doesn't need to be a well-paying job, but *something*. Still, it's been more than two years now, and I haven't really done that."

"The woodworking—is that recent?"

"Yeah. I like doing something with my hands, rather than throwing around legal jargon."

"Would you ever work as a lawyer again?"

"No way."

She nodded at the coffee table. "You made that?"

"Yeah. I made a lot of my furniture."

"For someone who hasn't been at this for long, you seem to be pretty good, not that I know much about it, of course. Do you sell much of your stuff? You're not going to get rich, but you don't care about that. You could set up a website, and people could commission you."

"I do have a website."

He pulled out his phone and showed her, and she tried not to look horrified. She didn't want to insult him, but…

"Jake, that might have been cool in 1999. It looks terrible on a phone."

"It's not that bad."

"I can make you a better one." She navigated to the Moonbeam Messages homepage. "Obviously, your situation is different. You might not want to sell stuff online in the same way. It could be more focused on showing what you can do, then people would contact you to tell you what they're looking for. Instagram could be good for you, too. As a side job, I make websites for small businesses. Not so much anymore, now that the store is doing better…"

Oh, God.

She'd overstepped with all this unsolicited advice—she hated when people did that to her. (Her mom, after all, was the queen of unsolicited advice.) And he'd already been in a bad mood, though it didn't seem so bad now, as he absently played with her hair.

"Sorry," she said. "Ignore me. It's fine if woodworking is more of a hobby. You don't need a fancy website—"

"No, I *like* that you're taking it seriously."

Oh.

Just how she would have liked it, ten years ago, if someone had taken her dream to open Moonbeam Messages seriously.

"I'll pay you, of course," he said. "To set up a website and, uh, show me how to update it and use Instagram."

"You're a terrible millennial."

He laughed for the first time all evening, and it warmed something inside her. For a minute, they just looked at each other, and she wondered…

No.

"How did you quit your job with Colton?" she asked.

Jake looked down. "A part of me wishes it was something dramatic. Like, I walked out in the middle of a trial, but..." He shrugged. "It slowly got to me over time. At the beginning, I admired people like Colton, and feeling like I was someone important meant something to me. This successful man thought I could do a job for him. He'd take me out to dinner, and we'd go to expensive clubs and pick up women." He shot her a sideways glance. "I suppose you should know that. There was a time when it was all a game to me. Picking up women, bringing them back to my condo."

"I can see you being very successful at it."

"Yes, well. I was smoother back then, too." He paused. "I was working a lot but living it up the rest of the time. Then I began to burn out and get disillusioned. I felt guilty about how Colton's business used people, just to improve their bottom line a tiny amount. I used to blame people for their circumstances, for living in poverty—"

"Jake..."

"I know, I know. But then I came to understand how problematic my views were—I'm still working on undoing some of that thinking. Plus, my parents were sad that I never had time for them, and Lewis was pissed at me, particularly about the resort Colton built up north, near a reservation. I became disgusted with myself. Couldn't stand to look in the mirror and live in my own skin. So, I quit."

She put a hand on his cheek. "I know that can be hard, even when you're miserable. Changing the perception everyone has of you."

"Don't feel sorry for me."

"I'm not. I know what it's like, that's all. I quit my acceptable job, divorced my acceptable husband..."

She shifted so that she was sitting up, her legs stretched along the length of the couch, her back against the armrest; Jake was beside her, one leg parallel with hers, the other bent with his foot on the floor. She was squished between him and the back of the couch, and it probably didn't look comfortable, but somehow, it was very comfortable.

Except she felt like she was in free fall and had no idea where she would land.

Jake was supposed to help her forget. Escape. But as they spent more and more time together, it got complicated. Yes, sometimes she was a blissed-out puddle who could barely think, but other times, he helped her feel comfortable with who she was, and perhaps she did the same for him.

Yet that feeling itself was discomforting. She wasn't sure she liked someone seeing her so closely, especially someone who was just supposed to be a good time as she got over a breakup.

But she was over Colton, wasn't she?

She started to straighten up. Maybe she should go. It was after eleven, but it wasn't a far walk to the subway, and that was what casual sex partners did, right? They didn't spend the night every time. They didn't talk about themselves like this. Didn't share the sort of things Jake had just shared with her.

God, she was bad at this, like she was bad at many other things.

But that's not true, Sierra. That's not how he sees you.

She was about to get up, but then Jake kissed her. Differently from the way he'd kissed her when she'd walked through the door and he'd fucked her against the wall, but just as good. Certain parts of her body awakened at his kiss, remembering their earlier coupling, and when he moved on top of her and rolled his hips against hers, she lost all thoughts of leaving that night.

She was helpless to do anything but stay here and take him inside her, again and again.

~

That Thursday, after spending much of the afternoon in his workshop, Jake went to meet Sierra at Moonbeam Messages. When they exited the store together, she turned west on Baldwin and he turned east.

"Where are you going?" she asked.

"I drove. My car's on McCaul."

"Why did you drive? It's annoying to park down here."

He shrugged. "I have a surprise for you. Come, I'll drive you home."

She looked at him suspiciously, as though expecting him to give her a pet skunk or similar, but then she reached for his hand and started walking east.

He was so distracted by the feel of her hand that he almost forgot where he'd parked. When had he last held a woman's hand like this?

They reached his mini SUV, and he gestured for her to sit in the front. He drove toward her house, and fortunately, he found a parking spot right in front. Not that his gift for her was super heavy, but it was a little awkward, and it would be best if he didn't have to carry it far.

They exited the car. He stepped behind the trunk but didn't open it up.

"I didn't wrap it," he said. "Too much hassle. So you'll have to see it here."

"Okay, I'm ready." She closed her eyes, which was adorable.

He opened the trunk and took off the blanket covering the gift.

"You can open your eyes," he said.

She gasped when she saw what it was. "Did you make this for me?"

"Yeah. Nothing fancy, but I noticed you have lots of books and other stuff covering your desk. Thought you could use it."

It was a short bookshelf—only three shelves—but it should be more than enough to fit everything. Though now he wondered if he'd made a mistake and she'd see this as a sign that he thought she was messy.

Then she smiled and said, "I can't believe you *made* me something."

Was she thinking of Colton, who probably didn't even pick out the stuff he bought for women? He had an assistant to do such things for him.

"Yeah," Jake said, swallowing. "It's no big deal, it didn't take me that long…" He trailed off, wondering why he was saying all of this, why he needed to justify it when she seemed pleased.

Because it was just supposed to be "casual," he supposed, and "casual" probably didn't involve handcrafting things for the other person.

But, dammit, he didn't want casual anymore.

He didn't want to pretend he was anything but very, very serious about Sierra.

He loved her.

He'd been doubting himself for weeks, telling himself he couldn't possibly have fallen in love the moment he met her, but now he knew he hadn't been wrong, even if Lewis, the smart one, acted like it wasn't possible.

No, Jake was absolutely sure of what he felt.

"Jake?" Sierra said. "You okay?"

"Yeah." He felt like the ground was quaking beneath his feet, but he was okay.

"It would be better if you carry it. I'd probably end up banging it on something and I don't want to hurt it."

She was chattering on as though nothing had happened, and his brain struggled to comprehend how that could be possible.

Was he alone in his feelings?

How correct were those listicles about rebounds?

"Besides," she went on, squeezing his bicep. "You have bigger muscles than me."

He hefted up the bookcase. Sierra closed the trunk, then scurried ahead of him to open the front door to the house.

"Where do you want it?" he asked once they were in her bedroom.

She pointed to the wall across from the door. "There, I think?"

God, she looked so fucking cute. She was wearing jeans and a V-neck T-shirt that wasn't low enough for even a hint of cleavage—and he knew she'd say she didn't have much in the way of cleavage anyway, but all of her was perfect as it was.

He wanted to whisk her away to his cabin and spend a whole month making love to her, cooking for her, and walking in the woods with her, nothing to disrupt them. He couldn't give her a weekend on a private island, but he didn't get the sense she cared much about that.

"I feel guilty," she said, snapping him back to reality.

He frowned. "Why?"

"You made me this"—she gestured to the shelf—"and I haven't done anything for you."

That was like a sudden blast of January weather.

"This isn't a transactional relationship," he said.

She pursed her lips at the word "relationship."

She still balked at the labels, and he wasn't going to push it, not yet. He wanted to, now that he realized he'd been right about his feelings all along, but he'd wait a little longer.

"Okay," he said, his voice scratchy. "Well, you're making me a website, right? Give me a small discount, as you think would be appropriate."

"Alright. That's fair."

"Good." He pressed a kiss to the side of her neck. "I have another question for you. I have a cabin up north—would you like to go with me, maybe for the Canada Day long weekend? Not sure if that would be possible for you, work-wise…"

"How much roughing it does this cabin involve? Is there running water and electricity? I'm not a camping kind of girl."

His lips twitched. "It has basic amenities, and it's on a small lake."

"As long as your idea of hot sex in the woods doesn't mean doing it on a pile of poison ivy, that sounds good to me. No more than three nights, though, because I don't want to leave the store for too long. If we go over the long weekend, I might not have to close it at all—other than Canada Day itself—provided that Marisol can work Saturday and Sunday."

She didn't seem bothered by the idea of going away with him, so that was nice; it wasn't too relationship-y to her. Perhaps she just thought they'd fuck a lot—and he certainly intended to have lots of sex. A variety of images were already running through his brain.

But he wanted it to be more than just sex, and maybe he'd ask her then if she'd be interested in more. He didn't want to tiptoe around it for months.

"Or maybe," Sierra said, a mischievous smile on her face, "rather than giving you a discount, I could give you something from my store instead."

"Please don't say my alpaca has a secret twin sister."

"Alpacas aren't solitary animals, you know. They do better in herds. You should really have more than one."

"Do they need to be the same size? Can mini alpacas bond properly with giant ones?"

"Hmm." She took out her phone. "I'll have to do some research."

Why did he find it adorable when she did things like this?

"Later," he growled.

He tackled her onto the bed, and they didn't get up for a long, long time.

[23]

As Sierra sat in the sushi restaurant and waited for her ex-husband, her mood took a downward turn. It didn't have anything to do with Justin, however, but a different ex.

She'd been staring at a picture on her phone. She'd stumbled across it by accident on social media—it wasn't like she'd purposefully sought out pictures of Colton Sanders.

Or Megan Chen, author of the Sierra Wu books.

Or Connie Lin, star of the Sierra Wu movie.

Yet even though she hadn't been looking, she'd found a picture of the three of them at an event in Hollywood.

It wasn't, of course, the first time that Sierra had unexpectedly seen Colton Sanders with two Asian women. At least they were clothed this time.

And Colton wasn't dating Sierra anymore, so he was free to do whatever he wanted.

Not that there was any news linking him with Megan Chen or Connie Lin. There was just this single picture, and Colton had lots of connections. Possibly, he'd exchanged only a few words with these women.

But something about this creeped Sierra out. She hadn't seen pictures of him with movie stars before—though maybe that was just because she hadn't looked—and the fact that it was this particular actress, the one who played the character with Sierra's name...

It stirred up the thoughts she'd had when she'd caught him cheating. Had Colton only been with her because she was Asian and he'd been amused by her name?

He could have dated tons of other women. Ones who were better looking than her, more successful than her, wealthier than her—though he didn't need the money.

Sierra wasn't down on herself. She thought she was confident enough for a woman who was told on a regular basis that she wasn't meeting her family's standards.

But in this capitalistic society, Colton fucking Sanders stood at the top of the pyramid. He'd said it was hard to know who liked him for who he was, and who just liked his money and power. Yet she couldn't help wondering if he'd truly liked her for who *she* was. In fact, how could he have? He'd never known her all that well, despite how long they'd been together.

"Sierra?"

She jumped when Justin Ho sat down across from her.

"Sorry," he said. "I didn't mean to startle you."

She slid her phone into her purse, not wanting to discuss what she'd been looking at.

Justin knew she'd dated Colton Sanders, and he knew they'd broken up, but not any of the details. They only saw each other a handful of times a year; she retained a platonic—very platonic—affection for him.

"It's okay," she said, smiling at her ex-husband. "Nice to see you."

The waitress came around and they placed their orders. A few minutes later, she brought over a small bowl of miso soup for each of them, as well as their drinks.

"We're having a baby," Justin said.

Sierra choked and spewed her cocktail over the table.

"A *baby*?" She reached for some napkins. She'd made a mess of the table as well as her shirt, and she'd responded inappropriately to Justin's news.

But he wasn't upset. "I should have known better than to announce it while you were drinking."

"Congratulations," Sierra said. That was a more appropriate response, right?

It was a rather bizarre situation, hence her initial reaction. Justin had told her that he never wanted kids. They'd both been very clear on the matter. Their relationship never would have gotten far otherwise.

Now he'd changed his mind?

And how had she managed to get so much of her cocktail on herself? Just her luck that it was red, thanks to the cranberry juice, and her shirt was white.

"You look like Sierra Wu right now," Justin said. "In the movie, I mean." He snapped a picture and showed her. "You know how she's always wearing that white tank top with blood?"

Sierra looked at the photo on his phone. She could see his point.

She hurried to the washroom and attempted to clean herself off, but this shirt needed more than what she could do in a tiny restaurant bathroom. She resigned herself to looking like a mess and returned to the table.

"So," she said, "you're having a baby. But neither of you is in possession of a uterus..."

"Surrogacy," Justin said. "Our little boy will be born in three months."

She wanted to be supportive, but the knowledge that Justin had changed his mind about kids—getting a surrogate wasn't something that happened by accident—was hard to wrap her mind around.

"I really am happy for you," Sierra said.

"I know you're surprised. Don't worry, I'm not going to say you'll start dreaming of babies as well when you meet the right guy. But some part of me always did want kids—I was just convinced I'd screw it up. Had to spend a bit of time in therapy."

The waitress brought over the wakame salad. Justin smiled as he watched Sierra hungrily reach for some seaweed with her chopsticks.

"That's still your favorite," he said.

"Mm-hmm," she said around a mouthful.

"And Brussels sprouts?"

"You seriously think I'd stop liking Brussels sprouts? I haven't changed."

"You've changed," he said. "In a good way, don't worry. You're not trying so hard to have the life that your family wants for you." He studied her for a moment. "Are you seeing someone new? After Colton?"

"No. I mean, I have a fuck buddy, but that's not the same."

Of course, she just so happened to be in the middle of saying "fuck buddy" when the waitress returned to the table with their maki, which was a little embarrassing.

Ah, well. Sierra busied herself with pouring soy sauce.

Justin leaned forward. "I wish only the best for you."

"I know. Likewise." There was a slight ache in her chest. If only they'd been able to talk honestly to each other back then.

Had she really changed as much as he thought? Sure, she had her store, but she'd dated Colton partly because of what he represented—to society, and to her family.

She'd moved on, though. Had started moving on even before that infamous incident in the limo.

Her mind drifted back to the picture she'd found earlier, of Colton with Megan Chen and Connie Lin, and she clenched her chopsticks.

But she was okay. She really was. She had good friends and the little store she'd dreamed of, and she was on decent terms with her ex-husband. Yes, things hadn't been great in the aftermath of their marriage, but now, they could hang out as friends.

She even had a hot fuck buddy who was going to take her to his cabin up north. She'd been looking forward to that all week.

"Sierra?" Justin said. "What's with the dopey smile?"

"Oh, nothing."

And she kept right on smiling.

After having dinner with Justin, Sierra took transit home. As she approached her house, she saw someone on the porch, knocking on the front door. It was Weston, carrying an enormous vase of flowers, even bigger than the ones that Colton had brought by before. It looked positively ridiculous in his arms.

"No," Sierra said by way of greeting as she climbed the front steps. "I'm not interested."

Weston inclined his head toward the town car down the street. "Colton would like you to join him for dinner. I'll take you to him. He's very sorry—"

"I've already eaten, and like I said, I'm not interested. And if he wants me back, why isn't *he* here? Why did he send you, and why did it take him so damn long?"

"Colton was negotiating a big business deal. The most important of his career."

"And cavorting with Hollywood stars. Right. I sure do feel like a priority in his life."

"The deal's done, and he has time now to—"

"Weston," Sierra snapped. "No need to plead his case any further. Nothing will make me change my mind. I shouldn't have wasted as much time on him as I did."

Previously, she'd wanted Colton to want her back so she could reject him to his face, but it had been almost two months since their breakup. He clearly didn't care about her that much, and he'd sent his assistant to fetch her. Much less satisfying to pass the rejection through Weston, but she realized now that she didn't wish Colton were here in person. She was glad she didn't need to see him.

Weston, to his credit, didn't look shocked that a woman like her would turn down the great Colton Sanders. "I will relay the message," he said.

"Please don't come here again."

"I promise I won't."

"Thank you."

"Would you like to keep the flowers?" he asked. "It seems a pity to toss them."

Sierra shook her head and stuck her key in the lock. "Good-bye, Weston."

He nodded and headed down the steps, ridiculous flowers in hand.

She wondered if she'd hear—directly or indirectly—from Colton again. She sure hoped not.

$$[\ 24\ ]$$

She groaned. Why was someone disturbing her? She'd been having such a nice sleep.

"Sierra." There was a hint of laughter in Jake's voice. "We're here."

She opened her eyes, still feeling disoriented. It was dark, but in the lights of the SUV, she could make out the little cabin in the trees.

She bolted upright in the passenger's seat. "Did I sleep the whole drive?"

"Yep. Well, I shook you awake when I stopped to get food at Tim Hortons, but you told me to fuck off."

Shit. She *had* said that, hadn't she?

"I'm sorry," she mumbled. "I didn't realize I was so tired."

It was Thursday. Tomorrow was Canada Day. Jake had picked her up at Moonbeam Messages after the store closed and driven straight here.

"Was there lots of traffic?" she asked.

"It took four hours, which is longer than usual. It was pretty busy when we were leaving the city. Had to slam on the brakes a couple times, but you were blissfully unaware."

He got out of the vehicle and walked around to her side. He carried her into the cabin, and her half-conscious brain thought it felt like a groom carrying his bride across the threshold, though that was silly. They weren't even in a relationship.

He set her down inside the door and turned on the lights. She looked around as he returned to the car. There was a small kitchen, a living area, and two bedrooms. Nothing fancy, but that bed sure looked perfect right now.

"I don't know why I'm so sleepy," she mumbled. It wasn't as if she was working eighty-hour weeks, plus she'd had a vacation just a few months ago with Colton.

Though she'd stayed up a little late on Tuesday designing "new baby" cards, and last night, she'd finished Jake's new website… Okay, maybe she hadn't been sleeping enough lately.

"That's alright." Jake had returned with their suitcases. "You sleep. We'll have lots of time to do other things tomorrow."

"You mean sex?"

"Perhaps."

"Mmm."

She went to the washroom then collapsed in bed.

When Sierra woke up the next morning, she was alone, but Jake walked into the bedroom right after she sat up. He was wearing gym shorts and a T-shirt, and he looked delicious.

"What time is it?" she asked.

"Ten."

Wow. She really had slept a lot.

"I made coffee," he said. "It's probably cold now, but I can heat it up. You want some?"

"Sure."

He returned shortly with a chipped blue mug.

It was nice to have someone who looked after her in little ways. With the store, it was all on her—and she liked being in charge, but this was a nice change.

He sat beside her on the bed, and they were quiet as she drank her coffee. She was used to the background sounds of downtown Toronto, and it was so peaceful here.

"I'm still wearing my clothes from last night," she said.

"You look pretty good to me." He set down her mug and kissed her neck.

"Jake! I need to shower and brush my teeth."

"Alright. You do that, but then come right back to bed."

And that was exactly what she did.

They ate brunch at the picnic table behind the cabin. It wasn't super buggy, but there were still more mosquitoes than Sierra would like.

After that, she put on her bikini and Jake put on his swim trunks, and they sunbathed by the lake. She could see a few other small buildings dotting the lake, but it still felt like they were alone in a bubble away from the real world.

She hadn't needed to go all the way to a private island in the Caribbean for this.

Later, they went kayaking, something Sierra hadn't done in a very long time. She wasn't particularly good at, but it was fun, especially because she got to watch Jake's powerful strokes as he moved across the water.

After more lazing around by the lake, it was time for dinner. Jake said he'd take care of it, and soon the smell of burgers cooking on the grill filled the air, mingling with the scent of pine. In the distance, she heard a few birds.

"You like it here?" he asked.

"Yeah. It's nice." She sat down at the picnic table.

"My parents used to take us to this area when we were kids. I always wanted a little place of my own, so when I had the money..." He trailed off, perhaps thinking of how he'd earned that money. "Anyway, I've had it for six years, but when I first got it, I barely had time to drive up more than once a year. Last summer, I spent quite a few weeks here, though. Fixed it up a bit. I know it doesn't look like there was any recent repair work, but trust me."

"I'm getting hot and bothered thinking of you hammering boards onto...well, I have no idea what work you had to do. But the idea's still hot."

He chuckled as he flipped her burger onto a bun.

"Help yourself." He gestured to the condiments, then put a disgusting amount of ketchup on top of his own burger.

Which made her smile, actually. Was it weird to find something both cute and disgusting at the same time?

Sierra, on the other hand, put a *normal* amount of condiments on her burger before biting into it and groaning.

"Good?" Jake asked.

"So good."

He smiled at her, his eyes darkening as she licked some ketchup off her finger.

She couldn't help comparing this to other dinners she'd had on vacation, particularly those delicious multi-course meals on the tropical island. But somehow, this burger tasted better, even if she was eating it off a plastic plate and drinking wine out of a matching cup.

Yes, she was certainly enjoying it here.

She wouldn't lie to herself: she knew a lot of it was due to the man in front of her, the man who'd actually arranged this rather than hiring someone to do it for him.

It was easy to be with Jake. She could be herself around him, whereas with Colton, she'd always felt like she didn't belong and was two seconds away from screwing up in a major way.

"Is something bothering you?" Jake asked.

She shook her head, though a slight unease washed over her. Sure, there might not be a waterfall or grand terrace or pink sunset here, but it still seemed romantic. A little too romantic for someone who was just a fuck buddy.

She pushed that thought aside.

When they'd finished their burgers, Jake went inside and came back with dessert. She'd never been so excited by a grocery-store cherry pie in her life.

After lighting a citronella candle, he sat beside her, and they both dug in with their forks, eating right out of the tin. It seemed delightfully naughty. Something her mother would definitely scold her for, but her mother wasn't here.

Nope, it was just her and Jake, and it was perfect that it was just the two of them.

"My ex-husband and his husband are having a baby," she said.

Because, of course, she had to ruin the moment.

"Apparently, Justin always wanted kids, just thought he couldn't be a good dad. We were together for years, so I feel like I should have known that about him. Like, what does it say about me that Justin never felt comfortable enough to tell me…and that I was caught completely off guard by Colton's cheating?"

Jake hesitated as he had another bite of pie, and Sierra was anxious about how he'd respond. His words mattered to her.

"You're generally a trusting person and Colton's a douchebag, that's all, and you've said that you and your ex-husband just weren't right for each other. It doesn't mean anything bad about you, Sierra."

When he said things like that, her heart warmed.

This was what she wanted from her next relationship. The way it was between her and Jake—so different from what she'd felt in the past.

Yes, her next boyfriend would have a lot to live up to.

But she had time to look for him; she didn't need to rush into anything. And since she didn't want kids, she didn't have to worry about her decreasing fertility with age.

For now, she dipped her finger in the thick cherry pie filling and made a show of swirling her tongue around her finger. "Mmmm. That's sooo good."

As expected, Jake's eyes immediately zeroed in on her lips.

Then she dipped her finger in the filling again and slid it into her mouth.

She was wearing jean shorts and a striped tank top, her hair pulled back in a messy bun, licking grocery-store cherry pie off her finger, and she felt like the sexiest woman in the world, just because of how he was looking at her.

Yet, disappointingly, he still wasn't making a move. She'd have to continue this game a little longer. She stuck her finger into the pie once more, and this time, she threw her head back and touched her breast with her other hand while she licked her finger.

"For fuck's sake," Jake muttered.

The next thing she knew, he'd blown out the candle and thrown her over his shoulder.

Ooh, this was turning out even better than expected.

She laughed as he marched her into the cabin and set her down in the bedroom.

"Now don't move," he said. "*Anywhere.*"

"Where are you going?"

"To bring everything inside. There are bears, you know."

She wasn't the greatest at following orders, so when he went back outside, she shimmied out of her shorts and tossed them on the floor, followed by her tank top, bra, and underwear. Then she went back to stand in exactly the same place he'd left her.

He returned to the bedroom and prowled toward her. His hand slipped between her legs, running along her entrance and gently spreading her moisture. She pressed herself against him, needing more.

"You didn't listen to me," he whispered. "Now you'll have to wait until I finish the dishes." He abruptly pulled away.

"Jake!"

He just responded with a look. A stern look that made her even wetter than she'd already been, and any other retorts died on her lips.

She stood there, stark naked, as he left the bedroom and closed the door behind him. She could hear him turning on the water in the kitchen. Pictured him swirling the washcloth over a plastic plate, just as she wished he'd touch her...

Oh, he was an asshole.

She clenched her thighs together, but she wouldn't dare move any more than that, tough as it was. Her body was desperate for release, and he was washing the fucking dishes.

She shut her eyes and tried to breathe slowly, but that made her more aware of the cool night air on her bare skin and the throbbing in her pussy. Of how much she wanted something inside her.

He turned off the water, and she didn't hear it turn on again. What on earth was he doing? Was he drying the dishes, even though there was a dishrack? Was he going to do more cleaning, just to torture her for longer?

She didn't know how many painful minutes passed, but when the door to the bedroom opened again, she almost sobbed in relief.

"You doing okay?" He smirked as he walked toward her.

"You know exactly how I'm doing," she shot back.

He looked entirely too pleased with himself, and then his mouth crashed down on hers and his fingers dug into her bare ass, pressing her against his growing erection.

Oh, thank God.

He pulled away from her and stripped off his shirt. Then he walked her backward until her legs hit the bed and she toppled onto it, with him on top of her.

She arched against him. "Please."

"Soon."

He returned to kissing her, his tongue plundering her mouth as she hoped it would soon do a little lower. She kept squirming, loving the weight of him, but it wasn't enough.

When he stood up, she protested at his absence, though she did approve when he stripped off his jeans and boxers and took his cock in hand. The sight of this gorgeous man, touching himself while he looked at her, made moisture drip down her thighs.

"Put your finger in your mouth," he said. "Just like you did earlier. Give it a good lick." He waited for her to follow his instructions. "Then stick it in your pussy."

She moved backward to prop herself up on the pillows, then bent her legs and spread them wide before licking her finger. When she slid it inside her channel, they both groaned. His cock was leaking precum, and she wanted to suck it so badly.

"How's that?" she asked.

"Very nice," he said. "Very pretty."

Her gaze bounced between his face, his chest, and his hand fisting his erection. "Would it be prettier if I added a second finger?"

"No, you're not getting filled any more than that today. Not unless it's my cock."

"That hardly seems fair."

"Life isn't fair, Sierra. If it was, I'd…" He didn't finish, but he stepped closer to the bed, and though she'd already had sex with him more than once today, her desire was still overwhelming. "Now touch your clit with your thumb. Keep your finger inside you. How do you feel?"

"Wet."

"I love how hot you are for me." His voice was husky.

God, she'd never been as horny as she was around him.

"I think making you wait helped," he said. "I'll have to remember that."

"You're such a asshole."

There was a moment when she feared she'd said the wrong thing. Jake was trying to be a better person now—and maybe those words had gotten to him.

"In bed," she added.

"Only because you like it."

And that was true. Much as he was frustrating her, she knew it would be worth it.

"Touch your breast with your other hand," he said. "Stroke your finger over the tip. Pinch it. Yeah, like that."

He crawled onto the bed and pushed the hand between her legs out of the way, replacing it with his own. When he dipped his head, she cried out the instant his tongue made contact with her clit. She wasn't there yet, but she was close.

He spread her apart with his fingers. Licking and sucking… It was an overload of sensation. When she looked down at him, his head between her legs, there was a strange ache in her chest right before she came, gripping the sheets and pressing herself against his face.

"Please," she sobbed. "*Please.*"

She'd already come, but she needed his cock so, so badly.

He slid up her body and pressed a kiss to her forehead. A gentle kiss, in contrast to the way he kissed her when his mouth returned to her pussy.

She exploded again a moment later, and this time, when he crawled up her body, she wrapped her arms around him. His cock pressed between her legs. Hard and insistent.

He lay on his back and rolled on a condom. "Take a seat."

She lowered herself onto him, letting him fill her achingly slowly. Each additional inch felt like it was splitting her apart even more, but she didn't care. She needed this, damn the conse-quences. Damn the consequences of letting him inside her over and over, of letting him bring her to a secluded cabin and grill her burgers and buy her cheap cherry pie.

She raised herself up and sank down on him again and again, each time feeling even deeper than the last. She was sore from the fucking they'd already done today, but she kept riding him. Kissed him as they moved together. His fingertips dug into her ass and hips; they were both holding onto each other with everything they had for these few fleeting moments. The rawness of it was intoxicating and a little different from all the previous times.

He pulled out of her, and she was about to protest when he slid down the bed so he could lick her again, until she was writhing above him and barely able to support herself. Then he adjusted his position so he could thrust up into her once more, and she cried out into the quiet night as she collapsed on his chest and he spent himself inside her.

Afterward, he brought the rest of the cherry pie into the bedroom and they demolished it from the tin.

"You liked that, didn't you?" he said.

"Of course. But you better not make me wait like that every time."

He chuckled. "I wouldn't be able to handle it, either. I could barely focus enough to wash dishes. The thought of you standing naked in the room, waiting for me…"

"You could have ended it at any time."

He shrugged and slid a bite of cherry pie into her mouth. "I enjoy watching you beg."

"Monster," she muttered. Fondly.

And then he was on her again, and this time, she didn't need to beg.

They got ready for sleep, and when she curled up against him in bed, she felt almost melancholy. It had been one of the very best days of her life, and now it was over.

Well, she certainly had high expectations for her next boyfriend, that was for sure.

And she couldn't help worrying they were impossible expectations.

~

When Jake woke up on Saturday morning, rain was beating on the roof and streaking down the window panes, and all was right with the world.

Usually, he hated rainy days at the cabin, and based on the forecast, today would be rainy until dinnertime. But it was different when he was here with Sierra. He wouldn't mind staying inside the cabin all day with her.

When she woke up and smiled at him like the missing sunshine, they had languid sex, followed by breakfast.

"What are your plans for the day?" she asked, draining her coffee.

"My parents' old board games are here. We could play one?" He gestured to the shelf.

"Ooh." She didn't pull out the box he'd expected. He'd thought she might have gone for Yahtzee or Boggle or Scrabble...

Basically, anything but Snakes and Ladders.

He raised an eyebrow.

"What?" she said. "I'm the master of Snakes and Ladders."

"Pretty sure it's all luck."

"I'm aware, but it was the only game I won somewhat regularly against my brother." Her expression dimmed for a moment, but then she set the box on the table and grinned. "I'm red. You're blue. Since I'm the youngest—"

"By two months." The other day, he'd asked when her birthday was.

"—I get to go first."

On her first roll, Sierra went up a ladder. On her third roll, same thing.

Jake, on the other hand, kept rolling low numbers and not

getting anywhere, and when he was finally halfway up, he landed on the biggest snake, which sent him back to the beginning.

He normally would have been more bothered by this, even though the game involved zero skill, but he enjoyed Sierra's light smack talk and her celebration when she won.

"Look at that, Jake! I destroyed you! How shall I celebrate? By talking about it constantly for the next hour?"

"I have a better idea." He picked her up and carried her to the bedroom.

When they were cuddling afterward, he nearly asked if they could call this a relationship. But what if she responded poorly? On one hand, he didn't think she would, because they were basically acting like they were in a relationship, and two months had passed since her breakup.

Still…

If she shot him down, it would be awkward to stay up here, just the two of them. She might want to leave right away, but there was still the matter of the four-hour car ride—no guarantee she'd sleep the whole time again.

It would best if he didn't say anything until they were back in Toronto. He could do it when he dropped her off at home.

The next day was sunny and warm, and they relaxed by the lake in the morning, then headed back to the city after lunch. Jake spent much of the drive rehearsing a few sentences in his head, over and over, but it turned out to be for naught.

Sierra was dozing when he pulled onto her street and saw… what the hell?

He was pretty sure he knew who was behind this, and his hands tightened on the steering wheel.

Goddamn Colton Sanders.

[25]

"Sierra," Jake murmured. "Wake up."

Drowsily, she opened her eyes. They were on her street, but not all that close to her house. Perhaps because there weren't any parking spots.

Or because there was a marching band.

Now she was wide awake.

"Shit," she muttered before throwing open the car door and jogging down the street.

She'd reached her house by the time she recognized what the band was playing: the soundtrack from the Sierra Wu movie. On the tiny front lawn, there was a table laden with pastries, champagne, and flowers. Two servers were dressed up as geishas, and Colton was arguing with Rose.

"She's away for the weekend," Rose said.

"Text her," he demanded. "Ask when she'll be back."

"Why don't you?"

"Because she blocked my number!"

Sierra wasn't against a public gesture of love, but it had to come from the right person, not some dude who'd cheated on her.

And why the hell were there women in geisha attire?

The marching band was also ridiculous, and though she'd generally enjoyed the movie, she didn't want to be reminded over and over of the famous fictional character who shared her name.

Rose looked like she was close to having a meltdown—she didn't cope well with stressful situations like this—and Sierra hurried to her friend's side.

"Hi, Colton," she said.

Colton held up a hand to silence the band, and Sierra took the opportunity to glance at the delicious-looking goodies laid out on the table. She hoped she'd still get to eat those.

"Sierra." Colton was wearing a tux and looked good in it, of course, although all Sierra wanted to do was kick him in the face. He turned to Rose, shooting her a *get back* look.

Rose sat down on the porch steps.

When Colton dropped to one knee, Sierra's heart sank further. Was he going to propose?

She'd enjoyed her weekend with Jake. Quiet hours by the lake, winning multiple games of Snakes and Ladders. Lots of sex.

And then she'd come back to *this*.

She didn't feel like dealing with it.

Colton took her hands in his. "I love you, Sierra. I didn't expect to fall in love, but I did. When I saw you at the bar and heard your name when you were carded, I was amused. And you were cute, so I pursued you."

So it had been about her name at the beginning.

"I didn't think it would lead to anything lasting," he said, "but you were fun and spunky, and you didn't care about my money. You refused it on multiple occasions." He paused. "It's lonely at the top. Few people understand that. I'd started questioning everyone's motives when they were nice to me, but I soon realized that you're genuine."

Poor little rich boy.

Sierra tried not to laugh.

"Though I didn't fully understand what I had until I lost it."

"You mean when I caught you cheating on me," she said, unable to stay silent any longer. She pulled back her hands. "Don't deny it. There were two naked women sucking you off."

A trumpet player snorted. "You didn't tell us you cheated. Are you going to say it's no big deal because it was only one time?"

Colton looked momentarily embarrassed, and Sierra couldn't help wondering—again—how many times he'd cheated and with how many different women.

"Yeah," said a clarinetist. "You just told us you were declaring your love and would throw a bunch of money our way for a couple hours of work. We didn't know she wasn't on speaking terms with you and you'd *cheated* on her."

There were mumbles of agreement throughout the band.

Colton ignored them and returned to staring beseechingly at Sierra. He grabbed some flowers from the table and held them in her direction, "I know I screwed up, and I'm very sorry, but if you give me another chance, I promise to do right by you."

She wasn't tempted, not at all. It didn't mean anything that he'd made a big gesture and apologized—Colton Sanders was still a slimy billionaire who didn't really understand her.

"Hey, Colton," said a man, whom Sierra recognized as one of Colton's assistants. Not Weston, though—Weston wasn't present today, apparently having kept his promise to not come here again. "Do you want me to call off the sky writers?"

Sierra burst into laughter, and because she didn't feel like looking at Colton's face anymore, she glanced at Jake, whose eyes were hard and fists were clenched.

He'd made her that shelf, and it had been way better than this.

"Tell them to wait," Colton said before turning back to Sierra. "Look at me, babe. Will you give me another chance?"

"Fuck you," she said. "You're an asshole who uses people and then complains about them using you. You claim you love me, but I'm not convinced. The only things you love are yourself and making money."

The trumpet player erupted in a peal of laughter.

"I think it's ridiculous that you want to go to space just to say you've done it," Sierra continued, "but at least that'll put you far, far away from me and all your employees who don't have bathroom breaks and get in deep shit every time they try to unionize. I never want to see you again."

The band broke into a rousing rendition of "Hit the Road Jack."

"Shut up!" Colton shouted.

Sierra had never heard him quite this angry before.

Okay, maybe that wasn't true. She'd heard him get pretty angry on the phone with other people, and because he was a rich white man who was considered a business genius, he could get away with yelling at people quite a bit.

But this time, she was involved.

"You heard her," someone growled. "She told you to fuck off. Leave. Now."

It was Jake, who'd stepped to her side. When Sierra turned to him, she noticed multiple people filming this shitshow on their phones. How wonderful.

"And who are you?" Colton sneered.

"You know exactly who I am," Jake said. "I used to work for you."

"You think you can give her more than I can?"

"In terms of private islands and jewelry? No. But the things that matter to her? Absolutely."

Sierra didn't like them talking about her like she wasn't here.

"We're together." Jake put his arm around her. "So, if you could leave my girlfriend alone, I'd appreciate it." The words themselves might have been polite, but his tone could cut metal.

Sierra stiffened at the word "girlfriend," but sometimes men wouldn't take no for an answer unless they knew you had a boyfriend or could see the ring. Jake was just pretending in an attempt to get Colton to back off.

Unfortunately, Colton Sanders was used to getting his way and didn't seem deterred.

Why was he so intent on winning her back? He claimed she was genuine and he lacked such people in his life, but she wondered if there was more to it.

Not that it mattered. Because she had zero patience for this.

Colton started to take a swing at Jake, and Sierra instinctively moved between them, but that turned out to be unnecessary because four members of the marching band abandoned their instruments and tackled Colton.

"Don't hurt him!" Sierra cried. Not because she gave two shits about Colton, but because he was a powerful man and she didn't want anyone to get in legal trouble.

Another eight band members made a wall between Colton and Jake. It was awfully coordinated, as if they'd done this before, but surely having to prevent violence wasn't a regular occurrence for a marching band? The first four band members eased off Colton but stayed close.

"You're not getting paid," Colton shouted.

"Yeah, don't pay us just like you don't pay your taxes," a clarinetist shot back.

Sierra muffled her laugh.

Colton's assistant helped him up. They argued quietly for a minute before the assistant led Colton into a nearby limo.

Once Sierra saw the limo speeding down the street, she felt such a rush of relief that her legs collapsed from under her.

The last half hour had been a bit of a blur to Sierra. Jake had taken her into the house and up to her bed. There was now a cool washcloth on her forehead and a glass of lemonade on her bedside table, and she was starting to feel more like herself.

"Thank God." Rose entered the room with a platter of Colton's pastries. "You're looking better."

"Yeah, I was just overwhelmed," Sierra said.

"I'll leave you two alone."

"That's not…"

But Rose was already gone.

Jake sat down beside Sierra, appearing more concerned than he needed to be. She'd been glad he hadn't stepped in until near the end, trusting her to say her piece, which seemed to have taken a lot out of her.

"Do you need anything else?" he asked.

"You've already asked me that ten times."

"You fainted."

"I did not *faint*." She put aside the washcloth.

"You collapsed into my arms."

"I didn't lose consciousness, but yes, it was good you were able to catch me. Thank you for being here and telling Colton that I'm your girlfriend, even though it's not true…" She trailed off as she noticed the look on Jake's face. "What?"

"It's nothing," he muttered.

"It's clearly not nothing."

"It can wait."

"Jake, I'm lying in bed like a sick patient. I demand you tell me now."

He sighed and scrubbed a hand through his hair. "I know you wanted something casual, and I agreed to it, but it doesn't feel casual to me. We see each other several times a week. We text all the time. We went away together for the weekend. And my feelings for you are certainly… I love you. I doubted it for a while, but now I'm sure of it. I love you, Sierra."

She'd never imagined that two men would declare their love for her in the span of an hour. Why on earth had Jake…

Oh, right. Because she'd demanded he tell her.

"So when I said I wanted something casual," she began slowly, "you were hoping to treat it like a relationship and change my mind?"

He shut his eyes. "I wasn't attempting to manipulate you. I truly doubted my feelings and wasn't sure what I wanted."

"The last thing I need right now is another relationship."

"But doesn't it feel like we're already in one?"

She shook her head vehemently. "No, I just kept thinking that when I got another boyfriend, he'd have a lot to live up to after you. I wasn't only thinking about the sex, but also... Oh *God*. You're right. We're essentially in a relationship."

In many ways, she was closer to Jake than she'd ever been to Colton. They communicated more often than she and Colton ever had, and in terms of feelings...well, there was certainly something happening in her chest right now.

How had she broken up with one guy and immediately found herself with another?

"No, no," she sobbed. "This is all wrong. I should be taking a few months to find myself again. How did I let this happen? Why am I so bad at life?"

Jake's expression remained serious and slightly pained. "You're not bad at life, and not everything happens the way it's supposed to happen. Have you been seeing anyone else?"

"God, no." That would be far too much work, and besides, the idea of being physical with anyone else made her recoil.

How come she hadn't realized her feelings earlier?

"When were you going to tell me?" she asked.

"Today, when we got back. Which is what happened. I just didn't imagine..." He gestured to the window.

"I feel like you're pushing me into it."

"I thought you could see where we were headed. I thought you felt..." He shook his head. "Fine, pretend it's nothing," he bit out, "just because it doesn't fit in your timetable."

She sat up in the bed. "I'm not pretending it's nothing, but a lot has happened lately, and I need more time to think it through. A few days without billionaires and marching bands turning up on my front lawn to get my head on straight, okay? I'm sorry, but I'd like you to go now."

"No. You collapsed. You need someone to look after you."

Sierra swallowed hard. She wasn't used to men taking care of her. "Rose is here. I'll text you before I go to bed to let you know how I'm doing, okay?"

Jake didn't say anything else; he simply nodded and headed to the bedroom door.

Sierra barely had time to exhale before Rose ran up the stairs.

"I just spoke to your mom," Rose said.

"You *what*? She called?"

"Yeah, she saw the video online—it already went viral—and when you didn't answer your phone five times, she called me. I assured her you're okay and asked her to give you some peace."

It was a good thing Sierra was in bed. She was feeling light-headed again at the thought of thousands upon thousands of people watching that video. She picked up her phone, which she'd had on silent, saw the number of notifications, and dropped it.

"Let's start eating those pastries," she said to her roommate.

But the expensive French pastries didn't taste as good as that grocery-store cherry pie.

[26]

If Colton Sanders can't get his girlfriend back, what hope is there for the rest of us?

Women are too picky these days. They have ridiculous standards.

Not wanting a guy who cheats? That's ridiculous? wtf is wrong with you

Colton Sanders getting rejected? Hahaha. Love to see it.

Sierra had been scrolling through social media and eating pastries for the last half hour. As it turned out, there were not one, not two, but three videos circulating, and Colton Sanders was trending on Twitter.

Rose, who was sitting beside Sierra on the bed, plucked the phone out of her hands. "You need to stop reading all these tweets."

"But many of them support me!" Sierra protested.

"And a lot of them say vile things. Don't do this to yourself."

"It's better than the alternative," Sierra muttered.

"Oh? What's that?"

"Thinking about what's happening with Jake."

"What *is* happening with Jake?"

Sierra threw a pillow at her friend. "He wants us to be a couple for real, I said I wasn't ready for a relationship—"

"But it seems like you're already close to being in a relationship."

"Yeah, but I told him I needed some time."

Just then, the doorbell rang.

"I'll get it," Rose said. "Nicole and Charlotte are coming, did I tell you? Amy's still in Silver River."

When Rose went to answer the door, Sierra grabbed her phone back.

There was a tweet from @WuMama888: *I hope your dick falls off @TheColtonSanders*

Her mom had also replied to lots of people who were saying bad things about Sierra. Ma was really on a tear, and Sierra was simultaneously touched and horrified.

Nicole came into the room and gave Sierra a hug. "Are you okay? There's still a bunch of people loitering on your street."

Sierra explained what had happened with Colton—though Nicole had already seen the videos—and also what had happened with Jake.

Then Charlotte arrived five minutes later, and Sierra had to explain it all over again as her friends scarfed down pastries and Rose made tea.

"I'm such a mess." Sierra sighed.

"Well," Nicole said, "your famous ex-boyfriend brought a marching band to your house, and your mother is on Twitter. You don't have to decide what to do about Jake yet."

"I don't just mean today. Things are always going wrong for me, in big and small ways, and it's not all bad luck. I'm never doing what I'm supposed to do, no matter how hard I try..." Sierra trailed off when Nicole's phone started ringing.

"Sorry, it's my grandma," Nicole said before answering. "Hi, Po Po... Yes... Yes... No, I don't think so... Fine, I'll ask her, but I don't think... Okay... *Okay*." She looked at Sierra. "My grandma wants you to be in one of her TikTok videos. I don't recommend you agree."

God, what a day.

Nicole ended the call and turned back to Sierra. "Yes, you've done some messy things, and you don't try to hide it, don't try to present a perfect image to the world—which is good, in my opinion. I think your bonkers family has made you feel like you're never enough, but you definitely *are* enough, plus you embarrassed a billionaire who desperately needed embarrassing. Maybe you could use more distance from your family for your own mental health."

Speaking of her family…

Sierra's phone rang. Her mom was calling again, and Sierra couldn't avoid her forever, but she'd try to make this quick.

"Hi, Ma," she said, perky as though nothing much had happened today.

"Who is that man standing next to you in the videos? Why don't I know about him?"

"Are you saying I should marry him and have his babies?"

"Aiyah!" Ma exclaimed. "You need to tell me about him first. What's his job? Is he rich? Is he cheating on you? Why didn't I know you had a boyfriend? You keep hiding things from me!"

"Look, I don't know what's happening with him yet, okay? When I figure it out, you'll be the last to know."

"You're being smart with me."

"I'm doing alright, thanks for asking. My friends are here. Go back to causing mayhem on Twitter or whatever you were doing. I'll talk to you tomorrow."

"I was not—Why are there so many terrible people online? Why are they saying such awful things about you?"

Sierra's lips twitched as she ended the call and looked at her friends. Though she still felt like a bit of a mess, she did have some good people in her corner. Her heart hurt when she thought of Jake, so she'd try to avoid thinking about him for now. She didn't feel up to it.

Maybe that was okay. She'd told him she needed time, and she could allow herself that.

Jake spent much of the week hitting the gym and going for long runs as he attempted to forget about his love life. It reminded him of three months ago, when he'd been trying to push aside his feelings for a woman who was dating another man.

He hadn't been successful either time.

But he also had something else to do this week, for which he was grateful. Someone had contacted him via the form that Sierra had put on his new website, and he had a commission for a coffee table and a set of end tables.

He wiped the sweat off his brow, took off his safety glasses, and stomped upstairs, where he grabbed a cold bottle of beer.

Quinton and his girls would be coming over soon, and Jake wasn't ready for his friend's visit. He wasn't in the mood to see or talk to anyone these days, but Quinton had insisted, probably thinking it was for Jake's own good.

Frankly, if people really cared, they'd leave him the fuck alone.

Jake was tired. He'd been sleeping like shit. After three nights of sharing a bed with Sierra at the cabin, he struggled to sleep without her next to him.

He hadn't seen her in nearly two weeks. He wanted to help her with whatever she was going through, but some of that was related to *him*. And so, he was keeping his distance, as she'd requested, and feeling sorry for himself more than he liked. He didn't deserve anyone's pity, including his own.

He didn't feel too guilty about Sierra anymore, however—Colton had proven himself to be an even bigger piece of shit, and

Jake was clearly better for her. And it wasn't like anything had happened until after her breakup.

Still, there were all those years Jake had worked for Colton. Maybe he should do more to atone for it.

Yes, he'd donated money to organizations that spent much less on administration than Colton's charities did. He'd done volunteer work. He'd helped journalists writing pieces on Colton.

He no longer felt that billionaires should exist in society.

The thing was, it was hard to really take Colton down, and the viral videos just proved that. Sure, they were a small blow to the man's reputation, but there had been many of those over the years. Colton was like a Whac-A-Mole, always popping back up. He kept getting richer. Kept doing more bad things.

Jake smiled faintly at the memory of Sierra rejecting Colton in front of a crowd, but he wished she hadn't had to deal with that whole situation.

And she still hadn't said yes to Jake.

God, he loved her.

He'd loved her since the beginning, even if that didn't make any sense. There were lots of things in this world that didn't make much sense; it was just the way it was. And he'd only come to love her more as he got to know her better.

If only…

He hated all this goddamn wallowing.

On the plus side, at least he'd figured out what he wanted to do with his life. He just wanted a quiet existence with Sierra and his small woodworking business—and helping her with Moonbeam Messages as needed. That was all.

But he didn't know if it could happen.

When his doorbell rang, he opened the door, letting in Quinton and his two daughters. Gabby rushed toward Big Freddy in the front room. Jake had brought down the alpaca to entertain the girls.

"Gabby," Quinton said. "Come back and take off your shoes."

Gabby pouted but returned to the entrance and allowed her dad to remove her shoes. Then she and Liv ran to the giant alpaca, which was larger than the two of them put together.

Quinton slapped Jake on the back as he entered the living room. He declined a beer and sat down on the couch. Jake sat next to him.

"How are you doing?" Quinton asked.

Jake debated using words, then shrugged and took a pull on his bottle of beer.

Words weren't really his thing these days.

He willed the beer to ease the ache in his chest, but just like last weekend—the last time he'd drunk—it had no effect.

"I think," Quinton said at last, in a careful tone, "the fact that she didn't immediately shut you down, despite everything that had just happened, is a good sign."

"Sometimes I think so," Jake said, "but then the next day or hour or minute, I go back to thinking the opposite."

"Of course, I can't make any guarantees. But just know that we're here, no matter what. To visit and wrestle your giant alpaca and—Gabby, stop trying to pull off his tail!"

Gabby pouted again but obeyed her father.

"I know," Jake said. "Thank you for being here, even though I was a turd in the past."

"Daddy, what's a turd?" Liv asked.

"Poo poo," Quinton answered.

"Poo poo!" Gabby shouted.

"Hope you're enjoying the entertainment," Quinton said to Jake.

Jake was opening his mouth to respond when the doorbell rang. He headed to the door. It was Lewis, and Jake tried to stifle his sigh.

He was not in the mood for this.

Lewis raised an eyebrow. "Can I come in? You don't look happy to see me, and it sounds like there's a bit of a commotion."

"No, no. Come in." Jake gestured him inside.

Lewis was silent for a moment, but once he started speaking, he got right to the point. "I'm sorry I told Mom that you have a girlfriend. I saw the video...*is* she actually your girlfriend now?"

Jake gave his brother a brief rundown of what was going on.

"Look," Lewis said, "I know we've had our differences, but I really am sorry."

"It reminded me of when I was eight," Jake said, "and you told on me for biking one block farther than I was supposed to bike without supervision. One block!"

"Yeah, I was a little shit sometimes."

"A stickler for rules."

"I won't deny it." Lewis managed a tight smile. "I'm not going to apologize for some of the stuff I said to you a few years back, though. I wasn't wrong."

Jake held up his hands. "I'm aware."

"But I promise to do better in the future. I know you're not the same as you were then, and I believe your feelings for Sierra now. I could see from the way you looked at her in the videos. Even if no one else was paying attention to that part, I noticed."

"I care for her...a lot."

Lewis nodded. "I'll stop being a pain in the ass whenever you try to talk to me. Mom is pissed at me for that." Before Jake could say anything, Lewis added, "I'm not here just because of her, I swear. Now, what can I do to make you feel better?"

Jake wasn't sure what to say. Nothing could make him forget about Sierra, not even for a minute—otherwise he would have found it by now.

Fortunately, Gabby broke the silence. "Ice cream!"

Jake stepped into the living room, where Gabby was vigorously patting Big Freddy.

"He says he wants ice cream!" she exclaimed.

"Alpacas don't eat ice cream," Quinton said, "but maybe little girls can eat ice cream today, for a special treat."

Gabby started jumping up and down.

"Okay," Jake said. "Let's all go out for ice cream."

Except when they arrived at the local ice cream shop, it felt like someone had it in for him. There was cherry pie ice cream, which made him think of Sierra even more, if such a thing were possible. He ordered it because he couldn't seem to do otherwise, even though chocolate peanut butter was right there.

As he licked his ice cream cone and watched Gabby and Liv make a mess, he wondered what Sierra was up to today.

[27]

"You haven't told me what's happening with the man in the video yet," Ma said.

Sierra sighed and helped herself to the taro dumplings. She'd known her mother would bring this up. "I don't know, okay?"

She was still taking time for herself, and as a result, she'd drawn lots of new card designs for her shop. The problem? Most of them were "Miss you" cards, with pictures of sad suns, sad raccoons, sad cups of bubble tea, etc. She didn't need more at this point, but anything happier seemed to elude her.

She did really miss Jake. Missed his quiet confidence in her. The elation she'd feel when he showed up at Moonbeam Messages. The simple pleasure of being in his arms.

Ma clucked her tongue. "You'll lose him if you don't make a move. He'll find another woman! Aiyah, you're so old, not married. Biological clock is ticking!"

Auntie Marlene looked smugly at Rachel. Yes, Sierra was the failure of the family, and she was so, so tired of feeling that way.

"Stop it, Ma," she said.

"But you are—"

"Ma! No more. You know how much I dread family dim

sum? I don't even like having dim sum with other people because it reminds me..." Sierra shut her eyes to ward off the tears. "Of how I don't live up to expectations. How I'll never live up to expectations. I tried so hard. I got an acceptable degree and an acceptable engineering job. Settled for a husband whom I didn't really love, but at least—at the time—he wanted the same things in life as me." The one thing she'd never been able to compromise on was having kids. "I was miserable, though. And still, it never seemed to be enough. So I gave it all up, but I guess I didn't completely give up caring what you thought of me."

She opened her eyes and looked around the table. Her dad wasn't paying attention, as usual. Po Po stared at her disapprovingly, of course. Lincoln ignored Sierra as well as his sons, who were wrestling. Lincoln's wife was occupied with the baby, who'd started shrieking. Rachel looked sympathetic. Her husband was curiously absent. Gung Gung appeared confused, but kind.

And Ma appeared even more confused, like none of Sierra's words made any sense.

Sierra wasn't surprised. Her mother had never understood her, however...

"Those tweets, Ma. They were the first time I ever felt like you had my back and cared about me as a person, rather than the daughter you wished I could be."

"Ah, what are you talking about? I defend you all the time."

"No, you don't. You're really just defending yourself, in your rivalries with your sister and your friends."

"Sierra." Gung Gung's shaky hand touched her wrist. He didn't speak loudly enough for the rest of the table to hear. "I am not disappointed in you, I promise."

Tears came to her eyes again, but she forced them back.

She wasn't sure what Gung Gung understood about her life, but she could believe that even if he did know exactly what was going on, he would still like her. After all, he'd been the one person in her family who'd supported her art when she was younger.

"But I do not understand." He frowned, and she braced herself for evidence that her grandfather's memory wasn't what it once was. "What is a tweet?"

She couldn't help laughing. "It's a thing on the internet."

"Okay." He nodded. "I do not need to know."

Sierra turned back to her mother, who was looking at her oddly.

"That was the first time you felt like I cared about you as a person?" Ma asked.

"Yes. You never listen to what *I* want. It never matters to you." Sierra waited a beat, half hoping Ma would contradict her and give some examples, but that didn't happen. "Why did you write those tweets?"

"What did she write?" Lincoln asked.

"Look her up. Her handle is WuMama888."

Po Po glared at everyone for taking out their phones.

"Aiyah!" Ma said. "I don't like when people hurt you."

"But *you* hurt me," Sierra said. "Every time I talk to you, I feel worse. Jake—the guy in the picture—he made me feel like I was actually good enough for once. I think I'm finally going to do what's best for myself and stop coming to every family meal. They just make me feel bad." Her chin wobbled, but she tried to hold her head high as she waited for Ma to speak.

Ma kept quiet for a long time. The fact that she didn't protest was a relief, but at the same time, it hurt. Was Ma finally deciding to respect Sierra's boundaries, or did she just not care how often she saw her daughter?

Sierra swallowed the lump in her throat. Her mother did love her and wanted good things for her…but it was like that had been twisted into an obsession with status and appearances.

Hopefully, it could be better between them one day, but Sierra wouldn't count on that happening soon.

Her gaze drifted to her other family members. Auntie Marlene still looked slightly smug, and it appeared Rachel had noticed the same thing.

Rachel straightened her spine, opened her mouth, and said something that Sierra had never expected to hear from her cousin.

"I'm getting a divorce."

The table erupted in chaos.

As it turned out, Rachel's children already knew their parents were splitting up, and from the sounds of it, Rachel's husband had been cheating, although she didn't explicitly say so. It *was* clear, however, that he didn't pull his weight when it came to basically everything in their marriage.

After dim sum, Sierra lingered with Rachel.

"I'm so sorry." Sierra hugged her cousin.

"I let it go on much longer than I should have." Rachel pulled back and gave her a watery smile. "Because I liked looking like the perfect family, even if it was far from the truth. I admired you, you know. For not going along with it to the extent that I did."

Sierra nearly laughed at the idea that Rachel had admired her, but she supposed things were never quite what they seemed.

She went home, only to find the Moonbeam Messages website had crashed, so she spent two hours dealing with that before heading out again.

By the time she arrived at Ossington Cider Bar, Nicole, Rose, Amy, and Charlotte were already there. Sierra was mentally and emotionally exhausted and very much looking forward to having a drink, plus those delicious Brussels sprouts. She placed her order as Charlotte spoke about her struggles with packing, as well as her new puppy.

"He's a menace to society," Charlotte said in a grumpy-but-fond way. "He demands constant attention, and when he didn't receive it, he ate one of my T-shirts. The 'My Feelings Are Purely Plutonic' one."

"I'm sure you can order another," Amy said.

"No, the place I got it from doesn't exist anymore, but it's not like I don't have lots of geology T-shirts."

Sierra's cider arrived, and she eagerly gulped half of it, not contributing much to the conversation as Amy talked about her trip to Silver River. While in her hometown, she'd told her parents that she was pregnant. Fortunately, her morning sickness was improving, and she'd only puked once on the very long drive.

Sierra knew she couldn't avoid her friends' attention forever, though. Eventually, their curiosity would turn to her.

They waited until she had her hot, extra-cheesy Brussels sprouts in front of her.

"So, Sierra," Nicole said. "How are you doing?"

"Okay, I guess?" Sierra replied. "I stopped looking myself up on social media all the time, and since it's been two weeks, interest in the videos has waned. Everyone's talking about that weird pigeon video instead. And I kinda told my mom off, and my cousin Rachel is getting divorced..."

"But how are you *feeling*?" Nicole pressed. "About yourself. And Jake."

"I...I don't know. I think he's better for me than anyone else I've been with, but..." Sierra shook her head. "I do miss him, and I get teary-eyed when I look at the bookshelf he made me. And the otter mug I sell in the store, the one I made him buy." She also occasionally looked at the raccoon card with his phone number, which she still kept in her purse. "Yeah, I miss him a lot."

"But...?"

Sierra speared a Brussels sprout with her fork and chewed it before speaking again. "I'm scared. I don't know what exactly I'm scared of half the time, but I am. I know he won't cheat on me and bring a marching band to my house in an attempt to apologize, but there are so many other things that could happen." She paused. "It was easy to move on from Colton—what does that say about me? I was even a little interested in Jake when I was still with Colton."

"Sometimes life is complicated," Nicole said. "It happens. You were trying to figure things out for yourself, and Colton was the one sleeping around, not you—he doesn't deserve your guilt."

"Still. It was a long-term relationship, and it hasn't been all that long since it ended. I don't feel sad, I don't miss him. I shouldn't be ready for another relationship, but…"

"Don't think about how you *should* feel," Amy said.

Amy did have a point, but it was hard for Sierra to completely let go of those *shoulds*.

I should get married. I should have kids. I should go to university and get a respectable career and do everything I can to make my parents proud, even though they don't care about who I am.

"But wouldn't it be smart to have some time to myself after getting out of a relationship?" Sierra asked.

"You've had a little time," Rose pointed out.

"It's completely different from when I broke up with Calvin," Nicole said. "I truly did forget who I was when I was in that relationship, and I really loved him—I was so naïve back then. But it always felt like you never expected it to last with Colton."

"Because he's super rich and well known and I'm…not."

"No. I don't think that's all of it. You enjoyed being with him at the beginning, but you weren't that upset when he didn't show up when he said he would. It was like you knew you weren't compatible. Don't get me wrong, I think it's good you didn't let him change you much. But it seemed you were maintaining some distance between the two of you, and I wasn't sure you actually loved him."

"Yeah, I didn't, but…"

But I do love Jake.

Holy shit.

That thought came to Sierra out of nowhere. Why now, and not in the last two weeks?

It felt like something that had been true for a while, but she hadn't been conscious of it, like her brain and heart were resistant to the truth, afraid of what would happen if it didn't work out with him.

There wouldn't be a viral video, but her heart would hurt more than it ever had before.

But Sierra hadn't let her fears stop her from opening Moonbeam Messages, and she wouldn't let them stop her from having something real with Jake Tong. Though the timing might not sound optimal, it wasn't like she was still hung up on Colton, and it wasn't like she was rushing into a relationship because she was afraid of being alone.

Plus, it was easy to imagine it working out with Jake. She could picture their future together, which she'd never been able to do with Colton.

Quiet mornings drinking coffee with no kids underfoot. Going up to his cabin for vacation. Him meeting her at the store at the end of a long week…

She hoped she had the store for years to come. Jake would support her vision of it, rather than trying to turn it into a big business that she didn't want. She knew she could count on his support, and he loved her for who she was, not the idea of her.

"By the look on your face," Rose said, "I'm guessing you've decided to go for it?"

Sierra nodded. "Thanks, everyone."

She looked forward to properly introducing her friends to Jake. She was confident he'd stay by her side the whole time, unlike a certain billionaire.

But it wasn't like Jake was a good man just because she had Colton for comparison.

As she looked around the table, she thought about how Jake wasn't the only person who'd believed in her. Her friends had, too. When she'd been miserable at her last job, they'd encouraged her to follow her dream. They'd been supportive after her divorce. They hadn't insisted that she'd regret not having kids.

She could have her friends…and hopefully Jake, if he still wanted this.

She had to talk to him.

But first, she'd enjoy the night out.

[28]

Jake started reading the article. Colton Sanders was accused of bribing some MPPs to—

There was a knock on his door, and he got up. Every time someone had come to his door in the last couple of weeks, he'd hurried to open it, hoping it would be Sierra. Last time, it had been a delivery person who'd gotten the address mixed up, and the time before that, a political canvasser.

But this time, it actually was Sierra. She wore jean shorts and a sleeveless pink top, which looked utterly lovely on her, of course. In her arms, there were two gifts wrapped in flowered paper as well as an envelope.

"Can I come in?" she asked.

He gestured her inside and tamped down his urge to pull her into his arms and kiss her. They needed to talk first.

She sat down on the couch in his living room, and her hand shook as she handed him the purple envelope. Inside, there was a card with an illustration of an alpaca. It had a sad face, and in its mouth, it carried a string attached to a heart-shaped balloon with the words "Miss you."

"Did you draw this?" he asked, tracing his finger over the alpaca, which looked strangely like Big Freddy.

She nodded.

He opened the card and read her message. *I don't want something casual anymore, not with you, the man I love.*

When he looked up, she was twisting her hands nervously.

"I'm not in the habit of having rebounds," she said. "I didn't have one when my marriage ended. But even if I'd had lots, you'd be my favorite."

Jake squeezed her hands before giving into his urge to kiss her. He was hungry for her, as always—but especially after more than two weeks apart. He slipped his hands under the hem of her shirt, but she put a hand on his chest and stilled him.

"I have a few more things to say," she told him. "I'm serious about not wanting kids, and I'm not going to change my mind. My ex did, but I won't. So that has to be okay with you, if we're going to stay together."

"It is. I want the same thing."

She smiled as she wrapped her arms around his neck. "I told my family off, kind of. Going forward, they'll still be part of my life, but a smaller part. I won't feel the need to attend every family gathering."

"I'll go with you. Whenever you want me to."

She looked unsurprised, as though she'd already known he'd do that.

"I'm sorry it took me a little time," she said.

"It's okay. I know that day was a lot."

"I worried it was a bad idea to get into a new relationship so soon after a breakup, but timing isn't always perfect." She slid a hand into his hair. "Please don't doubt that I'm entirely invested in you. In us. I just needed a couple of weeks, but I'm ready for this."

"We can take it slowly, if you like."

"I don't think I'm capable of taking things slowly where you're involved." She shot him a lopsided smile, then handed him the first wrapped box.

It contained an otter mug, identical to the one in his kitchen.

"We can have matching mugs for our morning coffee," she said. "I plan to spend a lot of nights here, you see."

"I hope that you do." His voice was a little rough.

"You don't view me as a giant mess, the way some people do. You simply appreciate me as I am, which I've never really had in a relationship before."

"And I haven't had a proper relationship in a long time."

"We'll figure it out together."

He smiled. "You've already helped me figure out that I do want to take my woodworking business seriously, and a few people have contacted me through the website you built."

"Yeah?" She grinned. "I'm so glad."

The way she was happy for him—it spread warmth through his chest. He may have avoided relationships for years, but he really, really wanted this, and he'd do everything to make it work.

She handed the other box to him. "Now open this."

It was a pie. Specifically, a cherry pie from a place called Happy As Pie, which he recalled was near Moonbeam Messages. His pants felt a little tight as he remembered what had happened the last time he'd eaten cherry pie with her.

She scurried to the kitchen to procure some forks. "Let's eat out of the tin again."

She picked up a forkful from the center of the pie, whereas he took a bite from the edge. He fed the next bite to her, and her groan of pleasure made his pants feel even tighter.

"It's better than the one I bought," he said.

"I agree, but that was still pretty damn good."

She put down her fork, and oh God, he knew what she was going to do next.

Sure enough, she dipped her finger in the cherry pie filling, then lifted it to her lips and made a big show of swirling her tongue over the filling that clung to her finger, her eyes on his the entire time.

Fuck, this woman knew how to drive him wild.

He reached for the bottom of her shirt, but she shook her finger at him.

"Uh-uh," she said. "I'm still eating."

"You can eat while you're half-naked."

"Really? You won't distract me?"

"Would that be such a bad thing?"

Before she could answer, he whipped off her shirt and made quick work of her bra. Then he sucked one nipple into his mouth, and she gasped.

Yes, the cherry pie was delicious, but she was the treat he wanted most.

He picked her up, and she laughed as he carried her up to his bedroom, where he spent a very, *very* long time with his head between her legs before he buried himself inside her.

Afterward, he made some tea, served in their matching otter mugs, to have with the remaining pie.

And that was how he and Sierra spent their first official day in a relationship.

EPILOGUE

Several weeks later...

SINCE IT WAS a few minutes before six o'clock and Jake could see a couple of customers inside Moonbeam Messages, he waited outside and pulled out his phone. A headline soon caught his eye.

MORE BAD NEWS FOR COLTON SANDERS

Really? To add to the video of him literally kicking a puppy yesterday?

People who didn't care about the bribery scandal—or Colton's poor treatment of his workers—had been up in arms about that video. It had been filmed by a former assistant, Weston, who'd since turned on Colton.

And now, apparently, there was also tax fraud.

Some of the news coverage made it sound like Colton just had bad luck and had played no part in these things, which wasn't true. Some people said he should be forgiven because, well, what about all the jobs he created?

Jake couldn't help thinking that some of this shit never would have happened if he'd still been working for Colton. Not that he could have prevented the man from kicking a puppy, but the bribery, which was apparently related to a recent business deal? He never would have allowed that to go down the way it had.

There was talk that the tax fraud might lead to jail time for Colton, and maybe it shouldn't make Jake smile, but it did.

He put away his phone. It was time to see his girlfriend.

Sierra Wu, Not a Demon Slayer, was fixing the display of washi tape in Moonbeam Messages when the chimes above the door tinkled and her boyfriend walked in.

Unlike the first time Jake Tong had walked into her store, she smiled. Then she flipped the sign on the door to "closed," wrapped her arms around him, and planted a kiss on his lips.

"Just give me a few minutes," she said.

By six thirty, they were out the door. Since it was a beautiful late summer's day, they decided to walk all the way to Ossington Cider Bar, which would take them at least half an hour. She reached for his hand and squeezed it.

Funny how such a simple touch could make her grin.

Jake was meeting her friends tonight. He'd gotten to know Rose a little, but he hadn't met anyone else, aside from the brief encounter at the dumpling restaurant.

Sierra had every intention of going there again after they left the cider bar. What could be better than midnight dumplings with her boyfriend?

Then tomorrow, they'd head to the cabin, and she couldn't wait to spend several days alone with Jake, away from the rest of the world.

They arrived at the bar as Amy, Victor, Charlotte, Mike, and Rose were being seated; Nicole and David arrived a minute later. After introductions and a little talk about the weather, Nicole asked Jake a rather serious question.

"Have you met Sierra's family yet?"

"Not everyone," he replied. "Just her grandfather, as well as her cousin and her cousin's kids."

Rachel had been in a bind for childcare one Sunday, and Sierra had offered to help. She'd been at Jake's at the time, and he'd driven the two of them to Rachel's house for the day. Jake had turned out to be a particular favorite of Rachel's son, mainly because of his baseball skills.

Sierra had only seen her mother once since she'd officially started dating Jake, as she was no longer attending every family event. And when Ma had attempted to double her phone calls to make up for it, Sierra had quickly shut that down.

The little digs at her didn't hurt as much as they used to, now that she was feeling more comfortable in her own skin, and Ma, though she still had a ways to go, seemed to be making an effort to treat Sierra better.

A meet-the-parents meal was something that Sierra would have to mentally prepare for, but with Jake, she could handle it. Maybe early this fall.

"David met my grandmother and cousin the first night I ever spoke to him," Nicole said.

"Mike met my parents when we were six," Charlotte said. "They were very excited when we found each other again. Perhaps a little too excited."

Rose was the only one of their group who didn't have a partner sitting across from her. Although she had a smile on her face, Sierra could tell that smile was brittle, as though Rose was very aware of the fact that she was alone—and didn't want to be.

Sierra squeezed her friend's shoulder and looked at Jake.

She hoped Rose would one day have this, too.

Sierra returned from the cabin the following Saturday evening. She and Jake were spending the night apart for the first time in a while, and she needed to do some laundry.

When she returned to her bedroom to get a second load of clothes, she glanced at the wooden box on her dresser and smiled. Jake had made it for her, to keep all the greeting cards and other small items he planned to give her. There were already a few cards in it, including one with otters holding hands as they floated on their backs.

She was about to head back downstairs when her phone vibrated in her pocket. A text from Rose.

I won't be home tonight. I met a guy, and we're going back to his place.

ACKNOWLEDGMENTS

Thank you to my editor, Latoya C. Smith, as well as my beta readers—Daphne Green, Adele Buck, and Michelle Nochomovitz—for their help with this book. The lovely cover was created by Flirtation Designs.

Thank you also to Toronto Romance Writers, plus my family, for all your support.

ABOUT THE AUTHOR

Jackie Lau decided she wanted to be a writer when she was in grade two, sometime between writing "The Heart That Got Lost" and "The Land of Shapes." She later studied engineering and worked as a geophysicist before turning to writing romance novels. Jackie lives in Toronto with her husband, and despite living in Canada her whole life, she hates winter. When she's not writing, she enjoys gelato, gourmet donuts, cooking, hiking, and reading on the balcony when it's raining.

To learn more and sign up for her newsletter,
visit jackielaubooks.com.

Donut Fall in Love

The Stand-Up Groomsman

Cider Bar Sisters Series

Her Big City Neighbor

His Grumpy Childhood Friend

Her Pretend Christmas Date (novella)

The Professor Next Door

Her Favorite Rebound

Her Unexpected Roommate

Kwan Sisters/Fong Brothers Series

Grumpy Fake Boyfriend

Mr. Hotshot CEO

Pregnant by the Playboy

Bidding for the Bachelor

Holidays with the Wongs Series

A Match Made for Thanksgiving

A Second Chance Road Trip for Christmas

A Fake Girlfriend for Chinese New Year

A Big Surprise for Valentine's Day

Baldwin Village Series

One Bed for Christmas (prequel novella)

The Ultimate Pi Day Party

Ice Cream Lover

Man vs. Durian

Chin-Williams Series

Not Another Family Wedding

He's Not My Boyfriend

www.ingramcontent.com/pod-product-compliance
Lightning Source LLC
Chambersburg PA
CBHW030819210726

48290CB00002B/661